The Secret of
Camp Whispering Pines

Samantha Wolf Mysteries

#2

TARA ELLIS

ISBN-13: 978-1507800515
ISBN-10: 1507800517

The Secret of Camp Whispering Pines

Models: Breanna Dahl, Janae Dahl, Brandon Pless
Photographer: Tara Ellis Photography

This particular story holds special meaning for me. For this reason, I have to dedicate it to my lifelong friend, Lisa Hansen. So many of the escapades we got ourselves into while at summer camp inspired a good deal of the storyline in The Secret of Camp Whispering Pines. But even more important was the unique friendship that can only be formed by the events shared while traipsing around in the woods, swimming in the mountains and riding horses through the wilds. We were never short on imagination, and while this sometimes got us into trouble…we always had fun!

I would like to give a special thank you to my beta readers: Linda Morris, Cindy Pierce and Lisa Hansen!

Samantha Wolf Mysteries

1. The Mystery of Hollow Inn
2. The Secret of Camp Whispering Pines
3. The Beach House Mystery
4. The Heiress of Covington Ranch
5. The Haunting of Eagle Creek Middle School
6. A Mysterious Christmas on Orcas Island

Find these and other titles on Tara's author page!

http://www.amazon.com/author/taraellis

Contents

Samantha Wolf Mysteries   iv

1. SUMMER CAMP!   7

2. WHISPERING PINES   17

3. CABIN NAVAHO   25

4. FIRST IMPRESSIONS   36

5. RUMORS   47

6. SINK OR SWIM   54

7. TRADITIONS   61

8. FAMILY SECRETS   72

9. LEGEND OF THE WOODS   84

10. DESTROYED!   95

11. ISOLATION   102

12. CREEK WALKING   113

13. SANDY   123

14. TRAIL OF DANGER — 129

15. THE MASK OF ZORRO — 135

16. SABOTAGED! — 147

17. PIECES OF A PUZZLE — 159

18. ANSWERS IN THE DARK — 166

19. THE TRUTH WON'T SET YOU FREE — 177

20. WHAT FRIENDS ARE FOR — 183

21. UNEXPECTED RESCUE — 193

22. REVELATIONS — 200

23. BARGES — 210

1

SUMMER CAMP!

The phone rings for the third time before Sam runs down the hall and snatches it off the cradle. "Hello!" she says loudly, flopping down in an overstuffed chair that sits next to a small desk. Grimacing at the archaic set-up, Sam feels a brief pang of frustration with her mom for refusing to give up on having a home phone. Even though the main reason is that their cell phones hardly work inside the house, it's still irritating.

"Sam!" the person on the other end shouts. "It's me, Ally. I've got a great idea for our next trip!" Sam smiles at her friend's unnecessary explanation. Of course, she knew immediately who it was! The two twelve-year-old girls have grown up as neighbors in their small, seaside town in Washington State. They are now best friends and inseparable. The first part of their summer has already proved exciting, visiting Sam's aunt and uncle at their inn in Montana. It involved a legend, ghosts, and treasure hunting! What could possibly have Ally all excited after going through *that*?

"Well, I really hope you *do* have a good plan," Sam responds, pulling her long, brown hair back from her face, and scooting to the edge of the seat in anticipation. "Because we've only been back home for a week, and I'm already going crazy. It's nearly impossible to go anywhere without fighting our way through the crowds!"

While nice and peaceful for most of the year, Oceanside erupts with tourists during the summer. The girls' normal hangouts are overrun with small kids dripping ice cream. Parks and beaches are crowded with hikers and sunbathers. The business owners love it, but for the local kids without anywhere to go that can't be reached by walking or biking…it's a pain.

"Not to mention," Sam continues, "that Hunter is on a roll this week. I think he's pranked me five times already."

Hunter is Sam's older, fourteen-year-old brother. He has seemingly dedicated his life to tormenting her.

"Come over now, and I'll explain everything," Ally says, a bit mysterious. "I can't wait to tell you!"

They live just three houses apart, so it's easy enough to go back and forth, but Sam isn't known for her patience. "Then *don't* wait. Tell me now! I have to watch the twins in less than an hour."

While Hunter might be Sam's torturer, the 'Tigger twins,' aptly named for their constant need to be bouncing, are the loves of her life. The two little girls adore Sam. Even though they are a constant challenge, she doesn't mind. Her mom quit her job as a teacher when they were born two years ago, so she could stay home and raise them. Although her dad makes good money as a commercial fisherman, it's seasonal work, so money is always tight.

Saturday night is bowling night, and Sam's parents are on a league with her aunt and uncle. They made an arrangement last year that, in exchange for Sam watching the twins *and* her two small cousins every Saturday, they would pay the monthly fee for Sam's cell phone. Her aunt and uncle would be showing up soon to drop off their kids and pick up her parents. She doesn't have much time.

Huffing good-naturedly at her best friend, Ally seems to relish the opportunity to draw out the drama. "It'll be easier for me to explain in person," she insists. "Besides, I've got a flyer I need to show you. It'll just take a few minutes, but I'm already babysitting Cora…so you *have* to come here!" Cora is a little girl that lives across the street. Ally often watches her on the weekends while her parents work.

A flyer? Now Sam is *really* curious, but rather than press for more information, she slams the phone back into its station and leaps from the chair.

"I'm going over to Ally's!" she hollers, as she runs through the kitchen, where her mom is preparing an early supper. "I promise to be right back!" she hastily adds, before her mom has a chance to protest.

Her mom's response is muffled as Sam slams the door behind her, but she knows that it was just an acknowledgement. Going to Ally's is such a common occurrence, it would be rare for her parents to say no. Her mom knows she can count on her to be back on time.

Skipping down a rough, cobblestone path, Sam veers off across the manicured front lawn and weaves through evergreens scattered along its edge, marking the property boundary. They have just under three acres, and the backyard is much less tidy. Her favorite spot is an old barn nestled up against thick woods in the far corner. She's spent many hours reading up in the loft, where the old hay still smells sweet. She's been begging her parents for years to get a horse, but although they have the space, they claim not to have the time or money to take care of one properly. She hasn't given up on the dream.

It takes less than a minute to cut through the neighbors' yards and race up to Ally's grand estate. Although Sam's house is modest by comparison, Ally's has a smaller yard, just under an acre. The inside is a starker contrast. Where Sam's is filled with children's laughter, bickering, and warm smells of homemade cooking, Ally's is quiet and expensively designed, with everything in its proper place.

Both of Ally's parents work full-time jobs. Her dad is an administrator at a nearby Boeing plant (where they make airplanes,) and her mom is an intensive care nurse at a large hospital a half-hour away. She has a sixteen-year-old brother, but ever since John got his driver's license, the girls haven't seen much of him. He's either gone somewhere with friends, at football practice, or holed up in his room.

Ally is often at home alone. While they usually hang out there because it's quiet and they have more privacy, Sam feels a certain sense of relief when she returns to her family and all of the chaos. Ally claims not to mind being alone, but Sam doesn't always believe her.

It's close to five o'clock when Sam raps twice on the door before letting herself in. Ally's mom insists that she doesn't need to knock, but it's a habit she hasn't been able to break.

"We're in here!" Ally calls from the media room, located at the back of the massive house.

Kicking her shoes off in the foyer, Sam then scurries through the granite-heavy kitchen, and into a space that any teenager would think was heaven. It's also the only room where food and playing is allowed. A pool table sits at one end, where there is a mini kitchen/bar and dartboard. At the other end is an 80-inch flat screen TV, facing an overstuffed, U-shaped leather couch. The walls are lined with custom-made shelves, full of various games and other supplies.

Ally and Cora are in the middle of the room, surrounded by toys. The three-year-old is currently playing with a large pink pony, making it gallop across the floor with a doll flopping around on its back.

Jumping up, her not quite shoulder-length, wavy red hair bounces as Ally shakes a piece of paper at Sam. "You've *got* to see this!" she gasps, her blue eyes flashing.

Intrigued, Sam rushes forward to snatch the flyer from her. The first thing to catch her attention is the image of a horse. *Camp Whispering*

Pines is scrawled across the top. Pictures below it show groups of girls engaged in various outdoor activities, including hiking, swimming, archery, and horseback riding. Her excitement growing, Sam's smile suddenly turns into a frown when she sees the dates and cost of the camp at the bottom.

"Ally, you know I can't afford this!" she cries, slumping down, dejected, on the large couch. "There's no way my parents could come up with five-hundred dollars on such short notice. The camp starts *next* Saturday! Anyway, I doubt Mom and Dad would let me go, even if we *did* have the money. I'm still suffering from nightly lectures about our last outing in Montana."

Although she and Ally had basically saved her relatives at the inn this summer from bankruptcy, they were lucky to have achieved it without getting seriously hurt. Sam's parents called it lying to an adult, but she likes to think of it as more of…withholding certain information until it was necessary to share it. Sam knows she made some poor choices, and endures the criticism with the right amount of shame…but she doesn't regret it. Now she wishes her parents had let her accept the reward money her aunt had offered, so she could afford the camp. Her parents flat out refused, but instead agreed to an open invitation to visit the resort for free whenever they wanted. She has to admit that it really wouldn't matter.

Taking the pamphlet back from her, Ally joins her on the couch. Sam doesn't understand *why* Ally is still smiling.

"Of course I know all of that!" Ally says, tucking her legs up underneath her. "You know that my aunt is a troop leader for the Scouts, right?"

Sam nods silently. Ally's aunt has been trying to recruit them for the past two years. Both of her younger daughters are in the organization. After seeing the camp, Sam's wishing now that they had gone ahead and joined.

"Well, every year, each troop gets a certain number of scholarships donated, so that kids who can't afford it still get to go. She just came by a bit ago, dropped this off, and told me that she still has one available. The scholarship is yours if you want it, Sam!"

Digesting this information, Sam's hopes swell slightly, but then dim again. "That's great, Ally, but I'm not sure that will convince my parents to allow me to go."

"I know. I've got that covered, too."

Looking closely at her best friend now, Sam is almost convinced. Ally seems so positive!

"I already talked to my mom about it," Ally explains. "She said that she'll call your mom and explain what a good influence this camp will have on us. They teach leadership skills there, and reinforce responsibility and stuff."

Transfixed by the picture of the girl riding the horse through the woods, Sam allows her smile to widen. "Ally, I think you'd better ask your mom to make that call!"

2

WHISPERING PINES

Sam finds it hard to believe that just a week after their conversation, she and Ally are now on their way to Camp Whispering Pines. Their mothers had spoken at length about it, but it was the promise of good character building and supervision that finally won Sam's mom over. Well…that, and several unfair promises to Hunter. In exchange, he's babysitting the twins for her.

There was a mad rush to get their applications filled out and turned in on time, but Ally's aunt helped them get it done. The scholarship was approved for Sam, and everything fell into place.

Now they're in the back of an extremely noisy suburban, along with Ally's two younger cousins and three other girls from their troop. It's a three-hour ride deep into the Cascade Mountains. Sam is sitting on top of her pillow, with a sleeping bag on her lap. She's quite certain that their bags will explode out the doors when they're opened.

In spite of the cramped space and hectic atmosphere, she can't help but be caught up in all of the excitement. A week filled with hiking in the woods, swimming, boating, and of course horseback riding. It's pretty much a dream come true. Sam would have been happy riding in the back of a cow trailer.

They leave the ocean behind them and quickly climb up into the rugged mountains, scattered with volcanos. They get a glimpse of Mount Rainier, looking like a surreal mirage against the skyline, before its view is blocked by the lower hills.

The Cascades run north and south, dividing Washington State in half. There are several active volcanos within them, but the most well-known is Mount Saint Helens, which erupted over thirty years ago, in 1980. Obviously, Sam and Ally weren't born yet, but their parents experienced it as kids and shared their stories with them. Because of this, the girls know that the beautiful, snow covered peaks might *look* peaceful, but giants lurk within.

It always amazes Sam how fast the woods thicken and close around the car as they drive up the mountain pass. Her dad likes to take them up to the ski resort sometimes and go sledding, so she's familiar with this part of the trek. Craning her neck, she tries to look out the window at the towering rock face rising before them. Although it's a hot summer day in the 80s, there is still snow and ice at the higher elevations, far above.

Just before they reach the ski resort, a popular summer location for hiking, they turn off the main highway. A large, brown sign designates the paved road as a national park access route. After what seems like several miles, they turn onto a smaller, unpaved road.

"Almost there!" Ally's Aunt Cathy calls out happily.

Her excitement building, Sam strains against her seatbelt as she leans forward and tries to see out the front window. However, between her own sleeping bag and the other girls' heads and pillows, she can see very little.

"I think I'm going to burst!" she finally gasps to Ally, who is sitting quietly beside her. Looking at her best friend curiously when she doesn't respond, Sam notices that Ally doesn't look so hot. She forgot how much Ally hates long drives. The cramped quarters probably isn't helping.

"I need air," Ally finally groans, "and a bathroom."

Not to be deterred by her friend's mood, Sam starts to bounce eagerly in the seat. Well, as much as she can with the limited space that's available. "We'll be there soon!" she says happily. "We'll find you a bathroom first thing!"

The vehicle pulls into a large, graveled parking lot. They circle around other cars, vans, and busses, before finally coming to a stop. When both backseat doors open at once, several backpacks and pillows immediately fall out onto the ground. Sam smiles. This is exactly what she expected.

"Come on!" she urges Ally, when her friend moves too slowly.

Once they're out in the fresh, pine-scented air, Ally's color *and* mood improve rapidly. It would be hard not to be happy in the middle of such a beautiful place.

Sam turns in a complete circle, trying to take it all in. Even with the parking lot full of vehicles and noisy kids running around, the vastness of the woods and mountains dwarfs them. *I'm going to like it here!* Sam thinks, smiling broadly.

"Come on!" she says aloud to Ally. "Let's go find you a bathroom."

After donning their backpacks and gathering up the pillows and sleeping bags, their small group follows the other campers along a well-worn trail. The trailhead is marked with a small, discreet wooden sign that simply says, 'Whispering Pines.'

"It's a half-mile to the main lodge," Aunt Cathy explains. "I'll make sure you get to the right spot and are signed in before I leave."

Distracted by a small, gurgling stream that

parallels the trail, Sam absently nods in acknowledgement to Cathy, before leaping over it and then back again. Giggling, Ally's younger cousin follows suit, but her shorter legs don't take her quite far enough, and she ends up with a wet tennis shoe.

Slightly embarrassed by Cathy's disapproving scowl, Sam can almost hear her mom's voice lecturing her about being responsible and setting a good example. "Sorry," she mumbles before scrambling to catch up with Ally, who is trying to set some sort of speed-walking record.

"Wait up!" Sam chirps, coming alongside her friend.

"I can't!" Ally breaks off the conversation upon spotting a small building around the next bend. Running now, she dashes for the bathroom, throwing her pillow and sleeping bag at Sam as she goes. Squealing, Sam juggles the items, ultimately losing the battle and dropping *both* of their beddings on the ground.

When Ally reappears, Sam has brushed most of the pine needles off their stuff and devised a way to hold everything.

"Much better!" Ally breathes, wiping her damp hands on her jeans. "I never should have had all that juice before we left!" Tucking her unruly red hair behind her ears, Ally seems to notice their surroundings for the first time. "Oh my goodness! This place is amazing!"

The sun is directly overhead, highlighting the beauty of the woods. Butterflies float through the beams of light, landing briefly on wildflowers before coasting to the next small splashes of color. Ferns nearly as tall as the girls nestle at the bases of huge evergreens, blending into the bright, green moss that hugs the bark.

Breathing deeply while trying to distinguish the different smells, Sam closes her eyes and listens to the assortment of birds calling to each other. She's brought out of her trance abruptly when someone grabs her arm. Opening her eyes, she finds Ally staring at her with a crooked smile.

"Come on, Pocahontas, we need to catch up with everyone. If we want to be in a cabin together, we need to sign in as fast as possible."

Laughing, Sam starts singing their favorite song from an animated Pocahontas movie as they run towards the large lodge just visible in the distance.

3

CABIN NAVAHO

It turns out that Ally's cousins hadn't been exaggerating during the car ride when describing Camp Whispering Pines. If anything, they had understated its size and impressive buildings.

Sam has never seen anything like it. The main lodge is a massive, A-frame log building with a huge front porch and sweeping steps. As they approach from the trail, the towering trees all around it make it appear smaller, but as they get closer, Sam's mouth hangs open.

A large open space in front of the lodge is filled with campers and their parents. Scattered around the clearing are other, more discreet buildings. Turning to study them, Sam walks towards the nearest one.

"Commissary." She reads the wooden sign hanging over a closed window.

"That's where you can buy extra supplies, like a toothbrush or bathing suit," Cathy explains. "You know, stuff you might have forgotten."

"They also have lots of candy!" her daughter adds happily. "That's why we bring spending money. The rope licorice is the best!"

Sam sticks her hand absently in her back pocket, confirming that the five-dollar bill she brought along is still there. How much licorice will *that* get her?

"Come on!" Ally urges, pulling her away from the little store.

On their trek across the courtyard, they also pass an office, a first-aid stand, and more bathrooms.

"Where's the swimming pool?"

Sam directs her question to Ally's cousin, who is walking beside her. Melissa is a year younger than they are, but this will be her second year at camp. Sam notices that she's still leaving behind one wet footprint in the dirt.

"Oh, that's over there!" Melissa points somewhere behind and to the left of the lodge. "You have to take another trail. But it isn't too far. We'll get to go swimming this afternoon! They have a required swimming test on the first day, to make sure everyone can swim. If you can't, you aren't allowed in the pool during free time, but only designated pool time, when there are extra lifeguards on duty."

Sam's not worried about a swim test; she and Ally are both excellent swimmers. Nodding to acknowledge that she understands, Sam then follows the crowd towards an area right below the steps of the lodge. Several tables have been set up so this must be where the sign-in is happening.

Linking arms with her, Ally pulls Sam a little closer in the swarm of girls, so that they won't be separated.

Sam isn't sure *what* she had expected, but this isn't how she had envisioned camp. That is, certainly not anything this big or organized. Her sole camp experience, aside from family outings, was a youth group retreat with her church a year ago. That had involved twenty kids and five big tents, and took place over the course of three days at a local state campground. This current scene resembles a kind of boot camp. As if to solidify that impression, a loud whistle pierces the air, making both girls jump.

"If you haven't signed in yet, please do so now!"

Searching for the source of the young, friendly voice, Sam finally spots a girl standing on the steps above them. She looks to be eighteen or nineteen years old. However, her long brown hair is in braids and she's wearing a Camp Whispering Pines T-shirt, making her appear younger. The freckles dotting her face, combined with her huge smile, cause Sam to relax a little bit.

Organized doesn't mean that it won't be fun! She tells herself.

"Don't worry," Aunt Cathy reassures them. "The first day is always a little hectic, but the girls *love* this camp. It's been in operation for over twenty years and is the best in the state!" Cathy's arms spread out as if she's herding chickens. She moves their group forward as one until they reach the tables.

The sign-in process is surprisingly quick

and simple. After their names are checked off a list, they are each given a black camp T-shirt with the initials 'CWP' on the back, and then directed to gather on the steps.

After Cathy says her good-byes, Ally's cousins and friends go to sit with their own age group, leaving Sam and Ally alone at the top of the stairs. They're more like bleachers really…that's how big they are, although made of wood instead of aluminum.

Ally stares down at the heads of several dozen girls sitting below them, varying in age from around ten to fourteen. Clasping the camp shirt tightly in her lap, she leans back against her sleeping bag, trying to blend in. Ally's never been shy, but this is a pretty big group of strangers. She might not feel quite so isolated if they weren't required to leave their cell phones at home. It is a camp rule. They hadn't worked while they were at Sam's aunt and uncle's earlier this summer, so she's already used to not having a phone all the time, but…well, she has to admit to maybe having a little twinge of homesickness. It would be nice to at least have the *option* of calling home if she wanted to.

Seeing the tense expression on her friend's normally happy face, Sam puts an arm around her shoulders and gives her a squeeze. "It'll calm down and be better once we get assigned to our cabin!"

"I hope so," Ally counters. "But what if we don't end up in the same cabin?" Her eyes widen. "I don't know w*hat* I'll do if that happens!"

Before Sam has a chance to respond, several whistles blow. Although alarming, it has the desired effect of silencing all the girls, and for that, Sam is thankful. Their attention now drawn to the counselors standing at the base of the stairs, she squirms on the edge of the step, impatient to officially start their next quest.

"Hello, everybody!" the same braid-wielding girl calls out, holding her hands out in a sweeping gesture. "Welcome to Camp Whispering Pines, where the fun never ends!" This must be some sort of prompt, because a large portion of the group suddenly starts singing!

Surprised, Sam and Ally first look at each other in confusion, but are then quickly caught up in the cheerful atmosphere and smile at the singing campers around them. It's a light-hearted song about campfires, hiking, and friendship. Sam finds herself tapping along with the tempo, and by the third time they sing the chorus, she joins in:

 "...at night, 'round the campfire, we laugh and we sing. We're here at Camp Whispering Pines, where everything is green. So come on and join us, for the time of your life. We'll hike, and ride and swim and sing all night...that's right!"

It's a silly little tune, but Sam and Ally find themselves standing with the crowd and linking arms. By the time they reach the end, they're all swaying to the words.

So *this* is what summer camp is all about!

Smiling broadly now, their initial fears at ease, they settle back down at the leader's prompting. It only takes one short burst of the whistle to regain control.

"My name is Butterfingers," she says, introducing herself. When this is followed by giggles, the teen takes it in stride and explains. "I'm one of the camp counselors and cabin leaders. We've all been given nicknames to make it fun." The teen gestures to the other counselors gathered behind her as she continues. "And so that it's easier for you to remember who we are. I'm a bit of a klutz and drop things all the time." Smirking at her own expense, Butterfingers turns to an older woman standing beside her. "This is our camp director, Ms. Cooper."

Sam can't help but notice that Ms. Cooper doesn't have a nickname. She doesn't look like someone who would allow one. Although wearing walking shorts, her camp shirt has been replaced with a more formal, buttoned polo with the delicate lettering 'CWP' stitched over the breast pocket. Her dark hair is pulled back into a proper, tight bun at the nape of her neck. It's hard to tell just how old she is. Sam figures she's around her mom's age. She suspects the lack of lines in the camp director's face may be due to a shortage of laughter, rather than years.

"Camp Whispering Pines has been in operation for twenty-four years," Ms. Cooper announces sharply, her words loud and crisp. "We expect you all to uphold our long-standing tradition of proper and responsible behavior. I hope you all enjoy your stay," she adds, somewhat unenthusiastically. Taking a step back,

Ms. Cooper makes it clear that she is done speaking. *Well...at least she's a women of few words,* Sam thinks.

"Okay, then!" Butterfingers shouts, rubbing her hands together. "Here we go. When I call out your name, please remain seated until I'm finished and then go to your assigned counselor."

Sam and Ally sit anxiously, listening to the third and fourth grade cabin assignments, then the fifth and sixth. By the time Butterfingers reaches the seventh grade cabins, the two girls are tense with the fear of being split up for the upcoming week.

"At this grade level, we group you together based on age," she explains. "This year, we have a larger group of twelve-year-olds, so we're putting them in the three upper-level cabins, and giving the thirteen and fourteen year-olds the teepees."

There's a chorus of cheers from the older girls and it's obvious to Sam that the teepees must be the most cherished accommodations. It doesn't make any difference to her *where* they sleep, as long as she and Ally are in the same cabin!

Finally, Butterfinger calls out her name as the first occupant of the third cabin. "In cabin Navaho, we have Samantha Wolf, Sandy Hollingsworth, Becky Johnson, Lexie Mills and…Allison Parker. And I will be your leader!"

At the sound of Ally's name, Sam hugs her friend tight. Both girls are so relieved to be together that they don't even cringe at the use of their formal names.

It's not long before rest of the list is finished. A mad rush of feet trampling down stairs begins as the campers all run to their new groups. The leaders hold up small flags with their crew names, but a few stragglers get confused, mostly younger kids.

After a brief moment of chaos, things settle down again. Sam eventually ends up standing next to Ally and three other girls, their bags and pillows piled around them.

"Cabin Navaho!" Butterfingers shouts cheerfully. "Follow me!" Without another word, she spins on her heel and heads for a dirt trail, leading up into the thick woods.

Excitement welling inside her, Sam and

Ally gather their things and scurry to catch up, convinced that a new, thrilling adventure awaits them.

4

FIRST IMPRESSIONS

After trekking uphill through the woods for several minutes in silence, concentrating on their footing, the campers break through into an open area trampled clean by years of use.

Butterfingers stops in front of the first cabin they encounter off to the right, the nameplate 'Navaho' clearly visible over the screened door. "This is home for the next week!" she says, holding the entrance open for them.

Sam looks fondly at a pair of chipmunks scampering into the woods, chattering as they go. She can just make out the outline of two neighboring cabins through the trees to either side. Her attention's drawn back to their own housing by the banter of the other girls picking out beds inside. Sam practically bounces up the two wooden steps and into the small structure.

"Sam!" Ally calls from a bunk bed in the far right corner. The walls are lined with them, one to a side, except for the front wall that accommodates the doorway and one full-sized bed and small dresser for the counselor.

Ally has chosen the bed farthest from Butterfingers, next to a window without any glass in it. In fact...*none* of the three windows have glass and there is a large gap where the top of the walls meet the exposed roof. No wonder they were advised to bring warm sleeping bags!

"I'll take the top!" Sam calls out joyfully, tossing her pillow up. Knowing that Ally always prefers a bottom bunk, she doesn't wait for confirmation. Pausing to look around the room, Sam sees that the other girls are having a bit of an issue, debating who will get the one bed that's left over.

"I have to sleep on the bottom, but I can't *stand* to have anyone sleeping above me!" Crossing her arms stubbornly, a feisty young girl flips her long blonde hair out of her eyes and squares off with her apparent adversary. Sam struggles to remember her name...something like Sandra.

"Why should *you* get to choose who gets their own bunk?" the other girl counters, but with much less attitude. Sam remembers her name is Lexie, because it's so unusual. She has close-cropped, black hair that goes well with her light complexion and spattering of freckles. She looks like someone who can handle herself, and Sam immediately likes her.

The last camper involved in the conflict is quietly sitting on the thin bottom mattress across from them. Hands folded in her lap, she is looking at the floor, her chestnut colored hair hanging down so that her face is obscured.

"Now Lexie," Butterfingers chides, having decided to intervene. "Do you really even care? If I remember correctly, you had your own bed just earlier this summer at the last camp session."

As Lexie turns to answer the counselor, Sam reflects on the comment. Lexie was at one of the earlier camps? How many times can someone go to camp in a summer? It would be fun to go more than once!

Blowing air out loudly between her lips, Lexie shrugs dramatically. "Naw...I don't mind where I sleep. I just don't think anyone should be so pushy, is all. How about you, Becky?" she continues, turning to the silent girl. "Do you care if you have your own bed?"

Shaking her head, Becky finally looks up at them all, eyes widening at the realization that she's now the center of attention. "I don't mind," she says, her voice stronger than Sam would have imagined. "But I'd like to sleep on the bottom...if that's okay," she rushes to add, her bravery seeming to waver.

Laughing, Lexie tosses her heavy backpack on top of the bunk that's kitty-corner to Sam. "That's settled then! You get your own pad, Princess."

"My name is Sandy!" she corrects, somewhat smugly. Obviously pleased with the arrangements, Sandy goes about carefully arranging her belongings, spreading them out on both the upper and lower beds of the last remaining spot, nearest Butterfingers.

"There you go, Becky," Lexie encourages.

"Get comfy! I don't usually bite, but I might talk in my sleep." Smiling now, Becky unrolls her sleeping bag and seems to relax.

"Sandy isn't very nice," Ally whispers to Sam. The two of them are seated on the top of their rustic framed bed, made from real logs. Legs swinging over the side, they have a great view of the situation.

"Maybe she just doesn't do well with being away from home," Sam murmurs back.

Not wanting to label anyone in the first hour that they're there, Sam decides to try to talk to her. Leaping down with a much louder thud than she intended, Sam blushes slightly but quickly covers it with a grin. "Hi!" she says to everyone, now that she has their attention. "My name is Sam, and this is my best friend, Ally. It's our first time at camp." She barely turns back from waving towards Ally, when Lexie grabs her outstretched hand and shakes it enthusiastically.

"Good to meet you! I've been to every camp session here for the past two summers, so if you have any questions about anything, I can help you."

Her first impression further solidified, Sam

nods at her new friend. "Wow!" she tells the slightly shorter, sturdy girl. "That must be so much fun. I wish my parents would let me do that." Pulling her hand back and shaking it slightly to get the circulation back into it, Sam notices the smile falter on Lexie's face.

"Yeah, well…that's not an issue for me." Without any further explanation, Lexie goes back to her bag and starts digging around in it.

"How about you, Sandy?" Sam asks, doing her best to sound friendly. "Have you been to camp before?"

Staring back at her through slightly narrowed eyes, Sandy folds her arms across her chest in a defensive gesture. "No, and I wouldn't be *here* if my mother wasn't forcing me."

Although rather short with a slight, frail build, Sandy is clearly someone who normally gets what she wants and isn't intimidated easily. She kind of reminds Sam of a Chihuahua - small, but fierce.

Turning away from Sandy's critical gaze, Sam widens her eyes at Ally in an "Oh my gosh" expression, before focusing on Becky, who is now spread out on top of her sleeping bag, a book to her nose.

"What are you reading?" Sam asks, sitting on the edge of the bed.

Slowly lowering the paperback, Becky looks back at her cautiously. "It's a mystery," she finally answers.

"Oh! I *love* mysteries," Sam tells her, turning her head so that she can read the title. It isn't one she's read before, but it looks interesting. "Can I read it when you're done?"

Deciding that Sam's interest is genuine, Becky pushes up to sit beside her and hands the book to her. "Sure, I should finish it in a day or two. Want to read the back?"

Happy to have found a mutual interest, Sam takes it and quickly reads the description. "It sounds a little spooky. I hope it doesn't keep us up at night!"

Grinning now, Becky places the book under her pillow. She's roughly the same size as Sam, but a little thinner. Her skin has a paleness to it that suggests she doesn't get out in the sun often enough. Sam instinctively feels protective towards the gentle, shy girl.

"We're all going to need these!" Lexie

interrupts, having found what she was looking for in her backpack. "The swim test is after lunch." She waves her swimsuit around in the air.

"I can't swim right after I eat," Sandy complains. "I'll get a cramp."

"You'll be fine," Butterfingers assures her, having just finished putting all of her stuff away in the only dresser. "We'll have time to come back to the cabin and get changed first. It will be a good hour before you're in the water."

Her fists clenching at the bedding, Becky gazes at Sam, panic-stricken. "I can't swim!" she whimpers, looking to Butterfingers for guidance.

"Oh…" Pausing, their leader chews on her bottom lip. "That's okay, Becky. It just means you can't swim during free time, but you can still go during open swim, which is twice during the week that you're here."

Hanging her head in embarrassment, Becky nods her understanding.

"I can teach you!"

Looking up at Sam's announcement, Becky's brows furrow. "How?" she asks.

"When is the first open swim?" Sam asks Butterfingers.

"Tomorrow. But it's only for three hours."

"Heck, I can teach *anyone* how to swim well enough to cross the deep end once, in just *two* hours!" Lexie says encouragingly. "It really isn't that hard, Becky. We'll help you," she adds, sitting down next to the two of them.

Her spirits lifted, Becky looks back and forth between Sam and Lexie. "Okay!" she finally agrees, and they all smile warmly at each other.

"Humph!" Sandy snorts. "Swimming in public pools is gross, anyways. Do you know how *dirty* they are?"

"Aren't you signed up for the creek walk in two days?" Butterfingers counters. Sandy stares at her boldly, bottom lip set. "If you want to participate in that," she explains, "then you're going to have to get wet. Passing the swim test is a requirement for it."

Her skepticism silenced, Sandy flips her hair defiantly before taking her swimsuit out.

"We need to get going," Butterfingers mutters, looking at her watch. "Lunch is in ten minutes. Put your camp T-shirts on, though."

A few minutes later, the five new cabin-mates emerge from Navaho and head back down the dirt trail. Sam and Ally linger at the back of the group, discussing their upcoming week's activities.

Turning towards Ally, who is walking beside her, Sam's distracted by a flash of light alongside the trail. Intrigued, she steps sideways and then onto the soft pine needles, to take a closer look. After a brief investigation, she locates a metallic plaque, attached to the trunk of an ancient-looking cedar tree, several feet into the woods. The flash she saw was the sun reflecting off it.

"What did you find?" Ally comes to stand alongside Sam, where she is crouched next to the tree.

"I'm not sure," Sam replies. "It says: In remembrance of our beloved benefactor, Mr. Harold Pine. May his legacy live on in Camp Whispering Pines. 2010"

"He's the millionaire who originally created this camp for his kids over twenty years ago."

Sam jumps at the unexpected voice near her ear, and finds Lexie leaning against another tree trunk behind them.

"This tree was supposed to have some special meaning to him, I guess," Lexie explains. "Something about how he proposed to his wife under it, before they bought the property."

"So now I get the Pine part of the camp name," Sam observes. "That's pretty clever. But why the 'Whispering'?"

"Because if you stand here when it's windy out," Lexie says hauntingly, "it sounds like someone is whispering in the woods."

"That's freaky!" Becky cries out.

Sam looks around Lexie to see the rest of the girls standing on the trail nearby.

"Come on!" Butterfingers interrupts, with more menace than Sam thinks is warranted. "Don't wander off anymore."

Feeling heavy under the ridicule, Sam and Ally step away from the memorial. However, nothing could keep Sam from digging into something mysterious, and she vows to find out the rest of the story behind the creation of Camp Whispering Pines.

5

RUMORS

As the Navaho campers near the lodge, others join them. By the time they get in line for food, the large room is filled with happy chatter.

Feeling somewhat overwhelmed again, Sam concentrates on selecting her meal from the huge array of choices. Finding the picnic-style table with the Navaho name on it, she and Ally finally sit down and look around. There must be a hundred other girls, as well as a couple dozen counselors and workers.

"How many people are at this camp?" Sam asks Lexie, who is sitting beside her. Butterfingers left them to go sit with some other leaders at their own table.

"Oh geez…good question." Tapping her teeth with a fork, Lexie looks up at the ceiling as she does the math. "I think there are three cabins for each grade, plus the teepees. So at six to a cabin, and the three big teepees, I would say just over a hundred kids. But I heard some talk last session about enrollment being down. Last summer there were *never* any empty beds. They filled up long before camp even started. My first year I almost didn't get in, and I registered three months before camp."

"We just signed up last Monday," Ally tells her, before biting into a big roll.

"I don't think they put us twelve-year-olds in the upper cabins because there are a lot of us," Lexie continues. "I think it's because they didn't have enough in the *lower* cabins. One of my younger friends said they closed down the whole third grade row and combined everyone else. Even advancing the thirteen-year-olds to the teepees, one's still empty. And I heard that four counselors were sent home because they didn't need them."

"Ally's aunt said this is the most popular

camp in the state," Sam counters. "How come enrollment is so low?"

"Well, it's just not what it used to be. Even in the past couple of years that I've been coming, it isn't as well organized, and there's been some…bad stuff happening."

"What kind of bad stuff?" Becky questions, her food apparently forgotten.

"I dunno if I should talk about it," Lexie hesitates. For once she seems at a loss for words. "I don't want to spread rumors and make things worse. I love this place and I want to keep coming here."

"Oh, who *cares*," Sandy interrupts. The four girls turn to look at her, shocked at the intensity in her voice. "My dad offered to *buy* this rundown excuse for a camp, and the board had the nerve to say no! So they can't be that bad off, can they?"

After a moment of confused silence, Sam is the first one to absorb the odd revelation and what it might mean. "Why would your dad want to buy the camp? And if you hate it so much, Sandy, then why are you here?"

Stirring absently at the corn on her plate,

Sandy looks like she regrets the outburst. Shrugging, she finally meets Sam's inquisitive stare and Sam is surprised to see tears shimmering in the other girl's eyes.

"Because I guess my dad's business needs a retreat, or a place to 'get away,' and when my mom came with him to tour this dump she fell in love with it. When the stupid Board of Directors for the camp voted it down, my mom *insisted* that I come here, because it's so *incredible*. She's hardly spoken to me for the past year, and suddenly she was so concerned about my....how did she put it? *Character building.* She was convinced Whispering Pines would be a good experience for me."

Stunned by the emotional confession, Sam looks to Ally for guidance, who's always a little better at being more sensitive with people.

"Maybe it won't be all that bad," Ally says encouragingly, reaching out to pat Sandy's hand.

Yanking her hand away as if a snake were about to bite her, Sandy stands suddenly and takes a step back from the table. Her face is a mixture of disgust and alarm at having opened up to the other girls. She spins around and flees the room, drawing some questioning stares from the other tables.

"Man…talk about a drama queen." Lexie watches Sandy leave and then shakes her head, returning to her food.

"I think it's sad," Becky whispers.

Falling somewhere in between the two views, Sam is experiencing a mixture of both irritation and sorrow. While she feels bad for the situation that Sandy is in, she thinks the girl's reaction really is overblown and a bit selfish. What she *is* sure of is that it raises more questions than it answers.

"What did you say to her?"

The harsh voice behind Sam and Ally makes them jump. Sam nearly falls out of her seat as she spins around to face Ms. Cooper, who is even more intimidating up close. Straightening up on the bench seat, Sam looks up at the tall, rugged form. Arms crossed, dark brows furrowed, the camp director is looking down her nose sternly at them.

"N…nothing," Sam stammers. "She was just telling us how her dad wanted to buy Whispering Pines, and she got upset about it, but-"

"Enough!" Ms. Cooper interrupts, cutting Sam off. "We don't tolerate gossip here, and you will do well to remember that!" Without another word, the director leaves in a huff, stomping loudly across the wooden planked floor.

"What was *that* about?" Butterfingers has joined them now, a concerned expression on her face.

The three new campers all look to Lexie for an explanation.

"I'm guessing Ms. Cooper's a bit sensitive with any talk about the camp being sold," Lexie suggests.

"Because she's afraid of losing her job?" Ally speculates.

"No, because she's one of the board members," Lexie says. "Her dad was Howard Pine."

"What?" Sam shouts. All sorts of new questions tumble in her head, but Butterfingers prevents them being asked.

"You need to respect Ms. Cooper's wishes, and *not* talk about this anymore. Okay, you guys?" Butterfingers turns to see where the older woman is, obviously worried. "Come on. We need to go get changed and head down to the pool soon."

The girls silently obey. As they begin gathering up their dirty dishes, they don't see Ms. Cooper step out onto the front porch. If they had, they might not have missed seeing her scowl turn into a satisfied smirk.

6

SINK OR SWIM

By the time they get back to the cabin and change, and then walk the mile or so of trails, they just barely make it to the isolated swimming pool on time.

Sandy was already in her swimsuit when they got there, and skillfully ignored them. None of the young girls had tried to talk to her, but Butterfingers had taken her outside for a few minutes before they left for the pool. Whatever was discussed seems to have helped calm Sandy down.

Now they're all seated on the wet cement next to the pool, lined up around its edges. They were sure to select a spot near the shallow end, so that Becky wouldn't risk falling into the deeper water.

The swim test is broken up into sessions, with the older girls going first. Butterfingers tells Becky that she needs to stay with the group, but can just pass when it's her turn to take the lap.

Sitting with her legs in the water, Sam is glad it's a hot day, because the pool doesn't seem to be heated. Although the pool is big, she can't imagine how they can possibly test all the campers in the time allotted. While considering this, she notices lifeguards in red swimsuits and shorts, standing opposite each other in the deep end of the L-shaped pool. There are six of them in total, four of them boys. Sam had been wondering if there were any boys there besides the kitchen crew and groundskeepers she had seen.

The oldest-looking lifeguard blows his whistle, and the girls fall silent. "I want you to form six equal lines behind each of us," he calls out in a deep voice. "There will be three of you swimming at a time, with the next girl entering the pool at the opposite end when a swimmer exits the water. You must be able to make it from one end to other, without assistance, to pass. Any questions?"

When nobody raises a hand, he blows the whistle again and waves them all into motion.

Contrary to what Sam had thought, the testing goes quickly. Before long, the shallow end of the pool is filled with campers who've passed. Ally is in line ahead of her, and she watches as her friend expertly dives in and does a perfect breaststroke to the other side.

As soon as she pulls herself up and out, Ally turns to watch Sam. The cool water is refreshing and she's eager to go join the other girls once Sam has passed.

Sam's dive is not quite as good as Ally's, and her stroke is not as sure, but she makes it across just as quickly. Smiling at her success, she stands next to Ally, slapping her on the back good-naturedly.

"Come on!" Ally urges, tugging at Sam's arm. They move off to the side, out of the lines of girls still waiting to go, but Sam pulls up just short of the shallow end.

"Wait," she calls to Ally, having to yell

over the squeals and laughter of the other swimmers. "Lexie is about to go. Let's wait for her."

Shrugging, Ally leans up against the wire fencing that surrounds the pool, letting the hot afternoon sun warm her cooled skin. *I might as well work on my tan!* she thinks, closing her eyes.

As Lexie dives in, Sam becomes aware of excessive splashing in the water close to her. Looking down, she expects to see a water fight, but is alarmed to instead find a young girl floundering. This far side of the shallow end bottoms out at six feet, according to the numbers painted onto the cement. There is a rope with floats blocking it off from the other area of the pool, but it's obviously over the distressed swimmers head.

Sam looks around frantically, realizing that none of the other girls can see what is happening. Spotting the only lifeguard still free to watch this presumably safe zone, Sam can tell that she has just noticed. Racing forward, the lifeguard leaps in without blowing her whistle first.

Grabbing Ally's wrist, Sam drags her over to the edge, pointing at the drama unfolding. The lifeguard has easily reached the panicked swimmer, but is having a hard time getting a hold of her.

Amazingly, no one besides a couple of other girls on the side of the pool has seen them. But they are both frozen in fear, mouths hanging open.

"Help!" Sam yells while pointing, struggling to be heard over all of the noise. "Somebody help them!"

One of the guards at the far end finally looks up, but Sam realizes there isn't time for the guard to reach them.

Sam has had basic rescue training as part of the swimmer safety course her parents make her take. She can tell that the young lifeguard isn't performing the rescue correctly. The struggling camper and guard are both going under for the second time, and they need help *now*.

Without a second thought, Sam performs a shallow dive and reaches them in just two strokes. Going to the young camper first, she approaches her from behind and hooks her arm around the thrashing girl's chest. Nearly drowned, most of the girl's strength is gone, so she gives little resistance to Sam as she drags her backwards towards the side of the pool.

Once there, Ally and two other girls pull the exhausted and terrified swimmer out. Sam looks back to see that the head lifeguard has his co-worker, and the two of them are already standing in the shallow water, where he towed her.

The whistles erupt all at once, signaling everyone out of the water. The rest of the lifeguards are all rushing over, and everything is in chaos.

Although more than able to get out on her own, Sam is helped by a growing crowd, and then becomes surrounded. Lexie and Ally each put an arm over Sam's shoulders, making sure that she's okay.

Everyone is congratulating her on the rescue, and her face burns with embarrassment at the recognition. "I just happened to be close by," she professes. "I'm sure you all would have done the same thing!"

"What is the meaning of this?" The booming voice somehow drowns out all of the other commotion, demanding attention.

The main lifeguard hurries to where Ms. Cooper is standing and they carry on a very animated conversation. It involves him first pointing towards the dejected guard sitting with a towel wrapped tightly around her, then the traumatized swimmer, and finally Sam.

"Butterfingers, bring that young lady to the camp nurse immediately!" Ms. Cooper orders, pointing to the lifeguard who'd had trouble.

"Alpine," the director continues, her voice harsh. "*You* will come with me!"

The young lifeguard, nicknamed for her height, hangs her head and leaves the pool area.

"The rest of you will carry on with your normal schedule. There is still another group waiting to be tested."

With that, Ms. Cooper makes a dramatic exit, leaving everyone exchanging glances.

Even with the sun hot upon her back, Sam feels a slight chill.

7

TRADITIONS

The rest of the swim time passes without further incident, and Sam is almost relieved when it's over. Normally, she loves every second she can get in a pool, but the atmosphere after Ms. Cooper's outburst was very somber.

After changing and re-grouping, Butterfingers tells them they have free time until dinner at six, over two hours away. "I'll meet you back at the cabin at 5:30," she says. "I have to run some errands now."

As soon as she walks away, the debating begins on what they should do with their afternoon.

"Let's go explore the camp!" Sam suggests. "I'd like to check out some of the trails."

"We aren't dressed for hiking," Sandy counters. "And I'm tired after all that swimming. Can't we just hang out at the cabin?"

Making a face at the boring suggestion, Lexie throws her hands up. "What we *need* to do, is get a head start on our barge."

"Our *what?*" Ally questions.

"Barge…a little boat. It's a camp tradition. We have to make it out of natural items found in the woods, except for the candle placed in the center of it. We all write a wish down on a small piece of paper to put on it. Then, at the end of the camp closing ceremony, each cabin launches the barge that they made into the lake. The last one still floating wins, and your wishes are granted!"

"That sounds stupid," Sandy whines, continuing her poor attitude.

"I think it might be kinda fun," Becky says softly. "How are we supposed to make it stay together?"

"Oh, there's an arts and crafts cabin that we get to use whenever we want, during free time. It's okay to use glue on it, but that's all." Lexie looks at Sam and Ally to see what their vote is.

While Sam would rather go hiking, she's curious about the barges, and the arts and crafts cabin sounds interesting. "Sure, why not?" she agrees, after Ally indicates that she doesn't care either way.

"Well, I'm going to our cabin," Sandy insists stubbornly. "I want to lie down."

"Suit yourself," Lexie tells her. She turns to walk in the opposite direction, the three other girls following her.

After brief hesitation, Sandy reluctantly chases after them. "I'm not about to go back to the cabin by myself. I'd probably get eaten by a bear or something."

Lexie tries hard not to laugh at the ridiculousness of her comment, but doesn't quite succeed.

"Go ahead and laugh!" Sandy scoffs. "I don't care, but I'm *not* helping with the silly barge."

Before anyone else has a chance to respond, Alpine dashes across the trail in front of them, clearly upset. She's changed from her red swimsuit and shorts into regular clothes, and has a big duffle bag thrown over her shoulder.

Coming up short, Alpine realizes she's almost walked right into the girls. They're on a narrow trail that leads into the woods behind the main lodge. According to Lexie, the staff cabins, maintenance sheds, and craft house are all back in here.

"Oh!" Alpine gasps, nearly dropping her heavy bag. She turns to Sam. "Aren't you the girl who helped me?"

"Yes," Sam confirms. "Are you okay?"

Alpine bursts out in tears at the question, letting her bag fall to the ground as she covers her face with her hands. Looking at the rest of her group, Sam is at a loss.

"Why don't the rest of you go get started with the barge," Ally finally says. "Sam and I will stay with Alpine."

Not needing any further convincing, the other three girls quickly head down the trail, leaving Sam and Ally to deal with the distraught lifeguard.

Sniffing, Alpine wipes at her nose and then

sits down on the bag, trying to compose herself. "I'm sorry," she whispers, hiccupping. "I've never been fired from a job before, and I was going to use the money for college. I graduate from high school next year. It wasn't even my fault!"

"You got fired?" Ally asks, shocked.

Sam isn't all that surprised, though. She knows that Alpine made some critical mistakes in the failed rescue attempt.

Nodding, it's obvious that the teen is trying hard not to break out in fresh tears. "Ms. Cooper told me to pack my bags and leave immediately. I mean, I could understand if I was actually a lifeguard, but I was hired to be a counselor for the fourth graders. I'm not even certified!"

"Did she know that?" Sam questions, alarmed that a director would put anyone uncertified in a position like that.

"Yes. I *told* her that I was a good swimmer, but had never taken any certification courses. Since they didn't have enough kids at this camp session, they had to close down some cabins. She said I had to either take the open lifeguard spot or go home. I should have just gone home, but she insisted that I would never have to really do anything, that I could just sit in the shallow end and stop kids from splashing. But that girl almost *drowned*!"

"She didn't drown, though," Ally consoles her, "and everyone is okay."

Sam is trying to think of something equally encouraging to say to her. She is saved from the task by Butterfingers, who jogs up the trail towards them.

"Sam! Thank goodness, I finally found you. Ms. Cooper wants to speak with you."

Expecting that the conversation would be a positive one, congratulating her on helping to save the drowning girl, Sam doesn't understand the concerned expression on Butterfingers face.

"Okay…" Sam hesitates, looking to Ally, who also appears confused.

"Just go to the administration office," Butterfingers directs, shooing Sam back the other way. "I'll take care of Alpine. Ally," she continues, turning to her. "Where are you headed?"

"Um…to the craft place to work on our

barge," she explains, obviously wanting to go with Sam.

"Then get going. Sam will meet up with you later."

Dismissed, Ally offers a brief, reassuring smile to Sam before walking away.

Unhappy with the turn of events, Sam grudgingly treks back past the lodge and over to the office. A bell rings as Sam steps inside. She finds much nicer decor than expected. The small space is divided into two rooms. The front half has an unmanned desk facing the entrance. The only item on it is an old-style rotary phone. Behind that is a wall with one door, and a sign on it that reads, 'Director.'

Ms. Cooper opens the door in response to the bell, looking all business. "Sam, please come into my office."

Encouraged by her tone, but still feeling uneasy, Sam does as asked and takes a seat in the only chair offered. It's a tiny office, but very neat. Surprisingly, there is a computer on the oak desk.

"I think it important that we set some things straight, Miss..." she pauses, looking down at a folder that's open in front her, "Miss

Wolf. Here at Camp Whispering Pines we have a system that works. It's based on long held traditions centered on responsible behaviors. This includes: honesty, integrity, safety and respect. When someone violates one of these, the consequences are unfortunate for everyone involved."

Wiggling in the chair under the director's obvious scrutiny, Sam has no idea where the lecture is headed. What did she do wrong?

"Take young Alpine, for example," she continues. "I entrusted her with the lives of my campers and she repays me by lying about her qualifications. This type of conduct cannot be tolerated, so I was forced to let her go."

"But wasn't she supposed to be a counselor?" Sam inquires, sure that there must be some sort of misunderstanding. "She just told me that she wasn't even hired as a lifeguard."

A dark veil of emotion transforms Ms. Cooper's face, her eyes narrowing. Sam leans back as far as she can from the intensity of it. *Uh-oh.*

"You will do well to remember your *place,* Miss Wolf," she spits, her voice tightly controlled. "I don't expect you to repeat those lies to anyone else. Do I make myself clear?"

Nodding slowly, Sam isn't sure who she believes now. Not one to normally question authority, it sure seems like the director might be more interested in protecting her own reputation than Alpine's.

"Furthermore, it would appear that you have a problem abiding by our safety rules. This is an area that has very little allowance in it for violators, and I am sure you can understand why."

Thrown off by this change of topic, Sam looks at her, perplexed. *How could she possibly blame me for anything?*

"There were plenty of other lifeguards at the pool," Ms. Cooper says evenly, standing and walking slowly around the desk toward Sam. "You put not only yourself at risk by jumping in, but the other camper and lifeguards, as well."

"But she was *drowning*!" Sam practically yells, her fear momentarily forgotten. "I'm trained in water rescue, and I knew what I was doing. She had already gone under twice and the other guards were too far away!"

"My head lifeguard has assured me that he was there almost simultaneously, with others right behind him. It was under control and you acted recklessly."

Sam is so stunned by the accusation that she is at a complete loss for words. Tears spring to her eyes. *Did she act inappropriately?* Thinking back over the order of events, she recalls Alpine's face as she struggled with the smaller girl, and her yelling for help. *No! There hadn't been any time. She didn't do anything wrong!*

Ms. Cooper mistakes her show of emotion and silence as acceptance of the criticism. "Has your counselor explained our three steps of discipline to you?"

When Sam shakes her head no, she continues.

"Step one is the assignment of a chore to be carried out in lieu of free time. Step two is a day in our isolation cabin, and exclusion from the day's activities. Step three is expulsion from camp."

Sam's stomach knots up. It's obvious that she is going to be disciplined. It doesn't make any sense, but she's helpless to do anything about it.

Arguing her point certainly isn't going to get her anywhere.

"For your disregard of our safety regulations, and lack of respect for authority, I am scheduling you for clean-up duty after dinner this evening. You will perform this chore tonight instead of having free time. I hope that this reminder will enable you to enjoy the rest of your time here at Camp Whispering Pines without further…problems. You are dismissed."

Sam watches as Ms. Cooper strolls back around her desk, picks up the folder, and then turns her back on Sam to open a file cabinet. Numbly, Sam stumbles from the chair and back out into the bright sunlight.

Blinking rapidly as her eyes adjust, Sam looks around at the courtyard with a new perspective. She's been at camp for less than a day, and has somehow already managed to make an enemy out of the director. The quaint buildings suddenly look a bit spooky, and the surrounding woods menacing.

8

FAMILY SECRETS

Not wanting to explain what happened to everyone just yet, Sam decides to go back to the cabin, rather than find the craft hut. The quiet, solitary hike back there is relaxing and allows Sam to think clearly about things.

An hour later, a concerned Ally is the first one to find Sam lounging on her bunk, reading Becky's book. The other girls follow Ally in.

Lowering the paperback, Sam smiles down at her friend's upturned face and bright, blue eyes. Before even reaching Cabin Navaho, she'd made the decision *not* to let her encounter with Ms. Cooper ruin the rest of her trip.

"Are you okay? What happened?" Ally drills, not swayed by Sam's calm demeanor.

Sitting up, Sam jumps down and hands the book to Becky. "I hope you don't mind that I started reading it. I was careful not to lose your place."

"Oh, I don't mind at all!" Becky answers, obviously happy that Sam likes the book.

Sandy has the same sour expression as earlier, and sits down on her bed in a huff. Lexie rolls her eyes at her before joining Ally in front of Sam.

"Princess burned her finger on the hot-glue gun," Lexie explains.

Sam cringes a little at the nickname Lexie uses for Sandy. While she agrees with the title, it still might be hurtful.

"Are you okay, Sandy?" Sam asks, peeking around the two girls who are still waiting for an explanation. In response, Sandy sticks her finger in her mouth and glares back at her.

"So?" Lexie pushes. "What did Ms. Cooper say?"

"She doesn't think I should have jumped in to help," Sam says. "Then, I sort of yelled at her, so she got mad at me for that, too, and assigned me to clean-up duty tonight."

"You *yelled* at Ms. Cooper?" Lexie gasps. "She's usually nice enough, but man…she doesn't put up with talking back. It's bogus though that you got in trouble for saving someone's life!"

Ally takes ahold of Sam's arm and pulls her aside. "Sam," she whispers. "Was it bad? Are you sure you're okay?"

"I'm fine, Ally. I'm not about to let washing some stupid dishes ruin our fun!"

Reassured, Ally gives Sam a hug. Before Lexie can ask any more questions, Butterfingers arrives, looking worried. She scans the room, stopping when she finds Sam.

"Sam, I feel like I owe you an apology," she starts, sitting on her own bed. "I should have warned you before you spoke with Ms. Cooper. She's really not that bad, but the one thing that ticks her off is when kids give her an attitude."

"She didn't even do anything wrong!" Lexie complains. "Ms. Cooper should be *thanking* her, not making her wash dishes!"

"No," Sam interrupts. "It's really okay, you

guys. I think it's mostly just a misunderstanding. Butterfingers is right. I think Ms. Cooper would have only given me a warning if I hadn't yelled at her. I didn't mean to, but I was so stunned. It's not a big deal. I'll help clean up tonight and it'll be done and over with. Okay?"

Looking around at her four cabin mates, Sam feels better as they all agree with her. Even Sandy smiles briefly at her while blowing on the tip of her red finger.

"Good attitude, Sam," Butterfingers praises. "Now. Let's go eat some dinner and have a fun night! You have more free time activities this evening." She pauses before continuing, looking apologetically at Sam. "And then a central campfire later, where you'll be introduced to some other Whispering Pines traditions. But first, I better explain the camp expectations that Ms. Cooper told Sam about, and the disciplinary steps."

There are a couple of good-natured groans, but the girls all sit at attention while Butterfingers outlines the three progressive steps.

"Other than following the main rules, there are a few other things you need to know.

Make sure you *never* go outside of the camp boundaries during your free time. The trails are plainly marked. Another biggie is that there is absolutely *no* food left in the cabins. It attracts all kinds of wild animals and obviously, these cabins have gaps in the walls and no windowpanes, so it's easy for them to get in. If you buy any snacks at the store, be sure not to bring it back here. Oh…and no littering. If you see garbage on the ground, please pick it up. We need to all take pride in our camp!"

While assuring Butterfingers they understand, it's clear that they've all worked up a good appetite, and there isn't any time wasted in getting ready and going to the lodge.

Dinner is served in the same buffet style as lunch. The girls pile their plates high with food and sit down at the big, wooden table.

"Hey, who wants to go boating with me after we eat?" Lexie asks around a mouthful of food.

"So there *is* a lake?" Ally asks, clearly interested.

Sam would have normally beat her to it, but she is looking dejectedly at her mashed potatoes. No lake for *her* tonight.

"It's not huge," Lexie answers. "But it's big enough to take a rowboat or canoe out on. It'll take us about fifteen minutes to walk there. We can have a full hour on the water before we need to head back. Sorry Sam," she adds, when she realizes her new friend can't join them.

"It's alright," Sam says. "I can go tomorrow, right?"

"Of course you can!" Ally agrees. "How about you Becky…and Sandy? Want to go?"

"I can't swim, remember?" Becky replies.

"That's what life vests are for!" Lexie hollers, slapping Becky on the arm. It's clear though, that Becky isn't encouraged.

"Isn't there a game room in here somewhere?" Sandy says, craning her long, slim neck to see the far end of the big room. "We could stay here, Becky, and play foosball or something."

Becky seems surprised by the offer, but happily agrees.

Sam is glad to see Becky and Sandy getting along better, and it makes her wonder about Sandy. She thinks there's a lot more to her beneath the surface, and she hopes to get a chance to really know her…if Sandy will allow it.

Before long, Sam is saying goodbye to her friends as they go their separate ways. She then trudges back to the work area of the kitchen. Surprisingly, some very friendly staff members greet her. Two are adults, but there's one other camper. Based on her expression, Sam is guessing that she's also here against her will, and wonders what *she* did to deserve it.

"Hello there, young lady!" an older man with deep lines in his face and rough, calloused hands calls out. "You must be Sam. My name is Cowboy," he adds, reaching out to shake her hand. He has a firm, sure grip and Sam likes him right away.

"Come into my castle and I'll show you the ropes."

With that, Sam spends the next two hours scraping plates, loading and unloading the dishwasher, and finally stacking clean dishes.

The other girl never really says much, but Cowboy keeps up an entertaining dialogue with everyone the whole shift. By the time Sam gets to the final step of washing off the counter, he's leaning against the end of it, talking with a man who came in to retrieve the garbage. Sam has seen him around the grounds, working on various things.

"Did you tell Cooper that the refrigerant in the freezer needs to be filled?" Cowboy asks, folding his arms.

"Yup," the younger man answers. "She pretty much brushed me off."

"Brushed you off? Well, what do you mean by that? Is there someone coming out to fill it, or not?" Cowboy demands, unfolding his arms and rising to his full height.

"I mean she brushed me off! Said there's other, more pressing and costly issues that have to be dealt with first."

"Doesn't she know how 'costly' it'll be if the freezer stops working?" Cowboy complains, visibly agitated. "That's not like her. Normally, she'd be all over me for not making the request *sooner*."

"Yeah, well…she's been acting a little differently ever since the board voted a couple of weeks ago," the other man says, gathering up the garbage bags and loading them into his cart.

"Hmm," Cowboy murmurs, scratching at his scraggly chin. "Is she even talking to her sisters?"

"I dunno, but what I *do* know, is that Old Man Pine would be rolling in his grave if he knew…" Spotting Sam listening, the man cuts off the conversation abruptly. "Umm, see ya later Cowboy." He hurries out the door as Cowboy turns to face Sam, who is blushing at having been caught eavesdropping.

"I, uh-I think I'm done sir," she stammers, setting the sponge down next to the sink. "Is it okay if I go?"

Looking sternly at her for a moment, Cowboy's old face then breaks out in a smile. "It certainly is," he answers kindly. "I think that if you hurry, you can make it to the bonfire before it gets started. It's not quite eight yet."

Thankful that she isn't going to get a lecture about minding her own business, Sam returns his smile and hurries from the kitchen.

Following posted signs and a few hurrying campers, Sam finds her way to the central campfire without any problems. It's in the opposite direction of the craft hut, and the trail leading to it starts out directly behind Ms. Coopers office. Sam is relieved when she doesn't see the director on her way past it.

Ally runs to greet her as soon as Sam steps into the clearing, and then leads her back to where the rest of their group is gathered. They're all wearing jeans and sweatshirts and Sam realizes too late that she should have changed first. It gets cold in the mountains at night, even during the summertime.

"How was it?" Ally asks. They sit down on a log that faces the large, already roaring fire.

"Not bad at all," Sam replies. "Really. This great guy named Cowboy is in charge of the kitchen and he was super nice."

"Cowboy's my favorite employee here!" Lexie exclaims. "He works with the horses on the trail ride, too. Are you going on the overnight ride Tuesday?"

Both Sam and Ally bounce up and down excitedly at the question. "Yes!" they answer at the same time, and then laugh at themselves.

"How about the rest of you?" Sam asks, looking at Becky and Sandy. They both nod, although neither of them appears happy about it.

"Lexie," Sam says, turning to face the other girl. "I overheard Cowboy and this guy talking about Ms. Cooper being upset after the board voted. He had to be talking about the vote not to sell the camp. Why would she not be talking with her sisters because of it?"

"Because the board is made up of Ms. Cooper, her brother, and three sisters," Lexie says. "I'm guessing she's upset with them for wanting to sell the camp. I think she's worked here for most of her life."

"Why in the world would they even *want* to sell it?" Ally asks. "It's got to be worth a ton of money."

"That's not what *we* heard," Sandy interjects, causing everyone to look at her curiously. "One of the other girls at the pool said that Mr. Pine's estate is worth *millions*, but this camp is using it all up. That's probably why my dad offered to buy it. He's very good at working those kinds of deals. I don't think the camp was even on the market, but they almost sold to him, anyway."

Just then, Ms. Cooper steps into the firelight, the shadows playing across the features of her face. Pausing, she turns to look directly at them, her eyes dark.

"I don't think we should be talking about any of this," Becky states. "It's gossip and we've already been warned about that."

"I agree. This is a campfire! Time to tell campfire stories, and I've got a great one!" Lexie rubs her hands together for emphasis, and has everyone's full attention.

"You've all heard of Bigfoot, right?" she begins. The four girls all nod, but Becky already looks wary. "So the sightings started earlier this summer. There have been three altogether, each one happening closer and closer to the camp…"

"Oh please!" Sandy interrupts. "Don't you have something more original?"

"No, it's true! One of them even…"

Lexie doesn't get a chance to finish, because Butterfingers walks into the inner circle of campers and calls everyone to attention. As she starts to lead them all in a fun campfire song, Sam looks at the gathering darkness behind them with a little more unease.

9

LEGEND OF THE WOODS

The next morning arrives bright, early, and *very* cold. The night before was filled with dancing, singing and making s'mores. Sam was appalled to learn that Sandy had never had one and it was quite funny to watch her eat it for the first time.

Her encounter with Ms. Cooper seems like a distant memory, and she's eager to start their second day at camp. However, the warmth of her sleeping bag is holding her back.

"I can't believe how *cold* it is!" Sandy whines from under her covers. Last night, Sam had thought Sandy was silly for bringing an extra blanket with her, but now she's envious.

"I think I can see my breath," Becky adds in confirmation.

"Oh ya big babies," Lexie laughs. Swinging her bare legs over the side of the top bunk, they dangle in front of Becky's face. "You'll get used to it. Wait till you go polar-bearing. That'll toughen you all up! Anyway, once the sun warms things up, you'll be complaining that it's too hot."

Polar-bearing is another camp tradition, where you take a morning dunk in the frigid pool water before a half-hour work out, followed by breakfast. Lexie had somehow managed to make it sound fun, but now it seems more like torture.

"Count me out," Sandy mumbles, her face still buried deep inside her sleeping bag. "I'll see you guys at breakfast."

Plopping down loudly onto the floor, Lexie turns to face Sam and Ally. "How about you guys?"

Reluctantly, Sam drags herself out of bed and then pulls Ally up. The three of them coax Becky into going, but Sandy won't budge. Butterfingers is already gone, and they find her down at the pool helping to organize things.

It proves to be just as shocking as Lexie told them it would be, and they are all wide awake when they line up to exercise. It turns out to be a lot of fun though, and Sam is glad that they decided to do it.

Breakfast is as good as the other meals were the day before. When they file back outside and into the courtyard, where the sun is now in full force, they feel energized and eager to do something fun. Butterfingers excused herself early due to a bad headache, so they don't want to go back to the cabin and disturb her.

"Now what?" Sandy is the first to ask. At least she isn't whining.

"Can we go hike around now?" Sam is quick to suggest.

"I'd really like to see more of the camp, too," Ally adds. She's happy that Sam seems to have shaken off her rocky start, and she's eager to get things back on track. A fun hike through the surrounding woods would be just the thing.

"Maybe we can do that for a while and then go to the lake?" Sandy offers.

Sam looks at Sandy in surprise. It's a good

idea and Sandy actually sounds pleasant. Maybe the extra sleep she got this morning was good for her.

"I don't see why not," Lexie agrees, looking to Becky.

"Oh!" Becky gasps. "I'll do whatever you guys want. I'm so nervous about learning how to swim this afternoon that I can't even think about anything else!"

Sam had almost forgotten. The first of only two open swim sessions begins after lunch. If Becky wants to be able to use the pool during their daily free time, she'll have to pass it. The second session isn't until Thursday, and they all go home Friday.

"You'll be fine, Becky" Ally says with confidence. "You already know how to float and do the doggy paddle. You can even hold your breath and go under. It shouldn't take us long to teach you how to do the breast stroke." They had taken advantage of the extra time in the pool the day before to find out what she could do.

"Do you really think so?" Becky questions, as they start up a trail.

"Absolutely!" Sam reassures her. "We've

got three hours, and you just have to make it across the deep end once."

After climbing along nicely groomed trails for half an hour, they emerge on the shoreline of a decent sized lake. Sam was already impressed with the beauty of the place, but the scenic, tree-lined shoreline practically takes her breath away.

"Oh my goodness, this is gorgeous!" she exclaims, taking in the distant mountain peaks and even a small island situated near the middle of the lake.

"I knew you'd love it," Ally says, smiling. Even Sandy seems mesmerized by it, and is the first to walk down to the water.

"It's pretty warm," she observes, shaking her wet hands. "Too bad we didn't bring our suits."

"We're only allowed to swim in the designated area," Lexie explains. "They always have a lifeguard on duty during free time. But you still have to have passed the swim test, since there's only one guard. Sorry, Becky," she adds, turning to the other girl.

Before they get a chance to discuss swimming any further, they're interrupted by loud laughter and shouts from nearby. Following the noise back to its source, they find several girls playing an intense game of volleyball on a sandy court. It's quickly determined that all five of them like the game, and they agree to play the winner.

An hour later, they're worn out and wishing more than ever that they'd brought their swimsuits. Instead, they settle for going in up to their knees right there next to the court, splashing and chasing each other. Cooled off, they head back towards the main lodge, debating what to do next.

"We don't have too much time left," Lexie notes. "Why don't we work on our barge until lunch? We're basically going to be gone for the next three days doing other stuff, so we should try and get more done."

Sam notices Sandy looking at the small blister fading on her finger and grins. She hasn't even seen the craft hut yet, but it sounds neat.

"I think that's a great idea!" Becky approves. After saying it, she glances nervously at Sandy. The two of them seem to have formed some sort of unexpected friendship and it's obvious that Becky doesn't want to upset her.

"So long as no one lets me use the hot glue gun again!" Sandy laughs, shaking her finger in the air.

Relieved that they all agree for once, Sam realizes that Lexie is right. They won't have any more free time for a while. Tomorrow is one of the big activity days. They all had a list of things to choose from when registering for camp. She and Ally picked a daylong hike for tomorrow that includes a creek and 'fanny sliding' down some waterfalls. The overnight horseback ride is the day after. That will only leave them Thursday for their remaining free time.

"Who else is going on the creek walk?" she asks, hoping that all of them are.

"I wouldn't miss it!" Lexie shouts, leading the way back onto the trail.

"Well I would," Sandy counters. "I'm going on the kayak trip. How about you, Becky?"

Looking at each girl shyly, Becky shrugs. "The only thing that didn't require the ability to swim: archery."

"Nothing wrong with archery!" Lexie tells her. "I've actually done that one, too. It's lots of fun!" Becky smiles in response, and everyone relaxes.

Their mood is light when they enter the small, airy art hut a short time later. Like the other cabins, it has a screen door and the windows are open. Where it differs are the rows of shelves that take up the wall space instead of beds. And three tables fill the middle of the room. The art cabin is such an unexpected thing, out there in the middle of the woods, that it has a magical quality to it. It's been decorated with ivy and vines so that it looks like something out of a fairytale, and Sam loves it.

There's only one other group using it now, so there's plenty of space to spread out the items they've collected so far for the barge. Sam notes several impressive pinecones, some cool looking moss, a picturesque mushroom and some fern sprouts. The base of the barge is a solid piece of bark, but it looks small in comparison to the other items…and to the other barges lined up on one of the shelves.

"Umm…." Sam mutters. "It's great, but don't you think it needs to be a little bigger?" Lexie gives her a pained look while handing her a small slip of paper.

"Write your wish down on that," Lexie directs. "We tried to find a bigger piece of bark, but we aren't allowed to actually pull it off the tree. All the other cabins seem to have picked the area around here clean.

"Then let's go look a little again, a little farther away this time," Sam suggests. Thinking briefly, she smiles and then jots something down. Folding the paper over, she drops it into a cup marked 'wishes'.

They all agree to look for a sturdier base, and they're soon quite a ways past the craft area. Sam is leading the hunt, scanning the forest floor. There are several fallen trees, but their bark is either already gone, or all mushy and covered with damp mushrooms.

Climbing up a slope, the trail changes from well groomed to less traveled, and soon Sam spots a couple of small flags staked into the ground.

"This is as far as we can go," Lexie points out. "Those are the markers."

They are at the top of the rise, and Sam can see for some distance. Twenty feet ahead is a large tree that looks as if it hasn't been on the ground for very long. Big chunks of bark are hanging from it.

"Stay here," Sam instructs. "I'll grab some of that bark real quick and come right back.

"I don't know if you should," Becky says, concerned.

"Nah, it'll be fine," Lexie decides, grabbing Sam's arm and pulling her towards the tree. "It'll just take us a second."

As they near the huge evergreen, Sam notes that Ally is following, too. By the time they come up alongside it, Becky and Sandy have also joined in on the escapade. Grinning, she's surprised at how close she feels to them all. Sam starts to pick up a good-sized section that's already on the ground, but nearly drops it when Sandy suddenly cries out.

"What?" Becky yelps, jumping back and almost falling down.

"I saw something!" Sandy whispers, pointing beyond them into a darker patch of trees.

"Stop trying to scare us," Lexie scolds, but she doesn't sound that confident.

"No, I really..." Sandy stops as a loud

cracking sound echoes around them. Something very big is moving nearby. Frozen in fear, they all turn towards the stealthy footsteps of someone…or *something* coming towards them.

"Who's there?" Sam calls out bravely, her voice cracking slightly.

The answer is complete silence. It's obvious that whatever it is…heard them.

Then, a large, shadowy figure leans out from behind a massive tree not more than fifty feet away. They all clearly hear deep, raspy breathing that doesn't sound as if it could come from a human being.

"Big…Bigfoot!" Becky barely chokes out, and her declaration moves them all into action. Turning as one, they blindly run through the woods, not daring to look back.

10

DESTROYED!

The mad rush back to Cabin Navaho is a blur, and Sam can hardly remember how they even got there. The first to arrive, she crashes through the screen door that's already ajar, and nearly falls over a backpack in the middle of the floor, its contents spilled everywhere.

Trying to catch her breath, she looks around in confusion at the destruction. Before having a chance to take it all in, she becomes aware of movement above her and looks up to find two *huge*, hissing raccoons perched on her bunk!

Already scared from the ordeal in the

woods, Sam's reaction is extreme. She screams in alarm, falling back. The rest of the girls run into the cabin, and Sam nearly collides with them, flailing her arms as she tries to regain her balance.

Ally reaches instinctively to catch her, but she's too late, and both of them go down in a heap. Convinced that Sam's screams and the cabin's disarray are signs that Bigfoot somehow got there before they did, Sandy, Becky, and even Lexie cry out and try to flee, but the screen door has shut behind them and they pile into it. This intensifies their fear, and they yell even louder.

"It's just raccoons!" Sam calls to them, pushing herself up from the floor. Her heart isn't pounding quite so hard in her chest now, and she's able to grasp what's really going on. Someone left the door open and the scavengers got inside. But why are they getting into her backpack? They have raccoons back home and she knows that while they're cute, they're nasty up close. They can also carry rabies.

This thought propels her the rest of the way to her feet. Maybe *that's* why they're tearing up their stuff in the middle of the day for no reason. Getting out of the cabin as fast as possible isn't such a bad idea.

Lexie spotted the culprits at the same time that Sam shouted to them, and is now holding the door for Sam and Ally, while keeping a close eye on the animals. "We'll leave the screen open and just wait for them to come out on their own," she explains, as they all gather out front.

"Wait for *what* to come out? What in the world is all of the screaming about?"

Sam groans inwardly at the sound of the director's voice. Ms. Cooper and Butterfingers have come *running* up the trail, apparently having heard the commotion.

Great. Just what we need right now. Sam runs a hand through her long hair, trying to gain some control of it so she doesn't look quite so desperate. As she does, Sam notices a long, bleeding gash on her right forearm. She remembers hitting it on something when she fell, but didn't realize it was that bad.

"We're okay," she offers quickly. "We were just surprised by a couple of raccoons when we got back. I was startled when they hissed at me, so I shouted at them. I'm sorry!"

Rushing forward with a look of concern,

Butterfingers reaches for Sam's wounded arm. "Did one bite you?" she gasps, looking a little pale.

"Oh, no!" Sam counters, shaking her head. "I tripped over some stuff and fell. It's just a scratch."

They're interrupted by a noise behind them and they turn to see the two creatures scurrying around the corner of the cabin and back into the woods. They don't look as big or scary now, and Sam is embarrassed at her overreaction. But she isn't about to tell the director that what had *really* scared them was the Bigfoot sighting in an area of woods that was off-limits.

Marching to the cabin, Ms. Cooper goes inside without even acknowledging Sam. Butterfingers motions for them all to follow, and they find the director standing next to Sam and Ally's bunk, hands on hips.

Turning to face them, Sam is alarmed by the dark scowl on her rigid face. "Still having a hard time following the rules, I see." She barks. It's obvious that she's talking to Sam.

"Wha-um, what do you mean?" Cringing

at Ms. Cooper's obvious scorn, Sam can't imagine what she's done now.

"Don't play games with me, young lady. Both you and Ally know the rules, yet you decided to keep *this* in your possession, a direct violation!" Holding her hands out dramatically, Ms. Cooper reveals a bag of cookies and two candy bars. They are a unique brand only sold at the camp store.

Ally's mouth falls open in shock and she looks at Sam in confusion. They've never even *been* to the store, let alone bought anything.

"That isn't ours!" Sam exclaims.

Reacting as if Sam had just slapped her, Ms. Cooper takes a step back and looks at her in astonishment. "How *dare* you lie to me!" she practically yells.

While the rest of her friends are cowering from the enraged director, Sam isn't having any of it. Placing her hands on her own hips in an imitation of Ms. Cooper, she squares off with her. "I'm not lying! I don't lie, and I don't make things up." Pulling the five-dollar bill from her back pocket, Sam waves it in the air. "This is the only money I brought with me, and I haven't even *been* to the store, so that *couldn't* be mine! If that was in my bag, then someone else *put* it there!"

It's clear at first that the older woman isn't sure how to respond. But it only lasts for a moment. Then her scowl deepens, her face reddens and she points a finger angrily, first at Sam, and then Ally.

"Both of you will clean this mess up. Then, you will check in with the nurse and get that scratch tended to before you report to the isolation cabin!"

Lexie gasps at this declaration, and Sam realizes that she has earned them step two of the progressive discipline.

"I would suggest that you *not* open that mouth of yours again," Ms. Cooper continues when Sam begins to protest. Her tone is menacing and Sam wisely obeys. "You will stay there for the remainder of the day, until bedtime at ten. This is your last chance, young lady. Unless you and Ally want to go home, then you had better learn to do as you're told. You're lucky that scratch *isn't* a bite, because then you would be on the way to the hospital to receive rabies shots!"

Becky moans behind her, and Sam feels bad for the other girl. Wait…she stops herself. This isn't even her fault. Sam can't believe that this woman is actually making her feel guilty for something she didn't do. What if her new friends believe that she's lying?

"There are valid reasons for the rules," Ms. Cooper presses, looking around at all of the upset girls, including them in her lecture now, too. "If you can't abide by them, then you *will* leave Camp Whispering Pines!"

11

ISOLATION

The silence in the cabin is heavy after Ms. Cooper leaves, and Sam and Ally stand there, looking at each other in disbelief.

"Come on," Butterfingers finally says. "Let's get this cleaned up, and I'll walk with you to the nurse."

Solemnly, they go about gathering up all of their belongings. A few items are ruined, but nothing worse than a sock and a hairbrush. Running her finger over the bite-marks on the handle, Sam turns towards their counselor.

"I really didn't…" she begins, but Butterfingers raises a hand, stopping her.

Frustrated, Sam looks instead to Lexie.

"I don't know *how* the food got there," Lexie states, "and I don't care. I just don't want to be dragged into all of this trouble. I *can't* go home," she says desperately. "Do you *understand*, Sam? I can't!"

Feeling horrible in spite of not being responsible, Sam simply nods.

Becky rushes forward and hugs her tightly. "I believe you," she whispers close to her ear.

Hugging her back, Sam is thankful for the support.

"Oh!" Butterfingers exclaims, addressing Becky. "I almost forgot. The archery program has been cancelled for tomorrow. You'll have to choose one of the other activities."

"Cancelled?" Ally asks, grateful for the distraction. "Why?"

"They didn't say," Butterfingers answers, somewhat irritated. "Just that it was due to unexpected circumstances."

"The only activities that don't require me passing the swim test are the little kid stuff!" Becky says miserably.

"Oh no," Sam groans, as it dawns on her

that they won't be able to go to the open swim session. "Ally and I can't teach you how to swim now!"

"That's okay," Lexie says, turning to Becky. "I can do it in no time. You'll pass that test today, and then you can go on the creek walk with us tomorrow!"

"Well, I have to know what you're going to do by dinner time," Butterfingers says, motioning to Sam and Ally. "We need to go. Let's get this over with."

Heads hung low, Ally links arms with Sam before following. But as Sam reaches the screen door, something *else* occurs to her. Moaning, she turns back. "I dropped the bark!" she admits. "After all of that, we don't even have the base for the barge."

"We'll find another one," Becky offers, when Sandy and Lexie remain silent. But she doesn't sound very confident.

Even more discouraged now, Sam is pulled down the trail by Ally, who is trying to keep up with Butterfingers' brisk pace. The counselor appears eager to get rid of them. Sam can't really blame her.

Approaching the nurse's cabin, located in between Ms. Cooper's office and the commissary, they overhear a loud conversation coming from inside.

"What do you mean, possibly *rabid*?" someone asks, the voice gravely. Sam assumes the voice belongs to the dark-haired, middle-aged woman Lexie pointed out yesterday as the camp nurse.

"That's not what I said," Ms. Cooper corrects. "It's just that these raccoons have been getting much more aggressive and bolder. I think it would be smart to check locally and make sure there haven't been any cases."

"If word got out that we might have rabid raccoons at camp, Whispering Pines attendance would decline even more!"

Looking thoroughly embarrassed, Butterfingers rushes to knock on the solid front door, causing the exchange inside to be abruptly cut off. Ms. Cooper yanks the door open and walks past them without a word.

"You'll have to excuse my sister," the nurse apologizes when they walk in. According to the nameplate on the desk just inside the door,

Nurse Angela Pine is indeed another one of the camp founder's daughters.

"You must be Sam," she says politely, turning and reaching for her arm. After a quick exam, Nurse Pine determines that all she needs is some antibiotic ointment and a bandage.

Once Sam is patched up and cleared to leave, they make their way to the back entrance of the kitchen, where Cowboy hands them two sack lunches. Obviously, he's expecting them and he eyes Sam questioningly. Humiliated, she avoids his stare, feeling like she's somehow let the older man down.

Each holding their small paper bags, Sam and Ally continue to follow Butterfingers in silence, heading now in the direction of the pool. Halfway there, they veer off the well-worn trail and onto a less used one. No more than twenty feet back, they arrive at a small hut. Sam remembers spotting it that morning on their way to polar-bearing. She had figured it was a storage shed and she's not far off from the truth. It's only big enough to hold one bunk bed and a card table with two chairs. Even then, it's extremely crowded.

Butterfingers simply holds the door open. "I'll send for you at dinner time. You'll get your food after everyone else, and bring it back here to eat. If you need a bathroom, use the one at the pool. But if you're seen doing anything other than that, or speaking with anyone, it's an automatic expulsion. Do you understand?"

When they both nod yes, Butterfingers turns to leave, but hesitates. Looking back, she has a mixed expression of anger and sorrow. It's obvious that she wants to say something else, but then seems to make up her mind and closes the door firmly behind her.

"Well, this is a mess." Ally is the first one to break the silence. Sitting down heavily in one of the chairs, she pulls her feet up under her.

"I just don't get it, Ally," Sam complains, sitting down at the little table across from her. "Who would have put that food in our bags, and why?"

Elbows propped on her knees, Ally interlaces her fingers and then rests her chin on them. "I've been thinking about that. Maybe it was meant as a harmless prank?"

"Maybe," Sam agrees. "Do you think that

might be the real reason that Sandy stayed behind this morning? She was the last one in the cabin, and she doesn't seem to like us very much."

"I'd hate to think so," Ally says slowly, "but she was awfully quiet after it all happened."

"I guess it doesn't really matter now," Sam decides, picking up a deck of cards from the table. "Ms. Cooper has it out for me and she isn't going to believe anything I say."

"I just hope she doesn't share this with our parents on Friday," Ally responds. At the end of camp on Friday night, the parents are invited to join them for the final goodbyes. Sam and Ally's moms have planned to come together and pick the girls up.

Sam has started dealing the cards for a game of War, but now pauses, closing her eyes. Plopping her forehead down on the table, she groans loudly. "Did you have to remind me? We'd never hear the end of it!" Looking back up, a card falls from where it stuck to her face.

Ally starts laughing, unable to stop herself, and, since the only other option is to cry, Sam joins her. Before long, both girls are sitting on the wooden floor, holding their sides from laughing so hard, the cards spread around them.

An hour later, they're into their fourth card game when the voices of dozens of campers walking down the nearby trail interrupt them. Going to the only window, they both peer out, watching for their friends on the way to the pool. They aren't able to get a clear view, though. Frustrated, they go back to their only form of entertainment.

After what seems like an eternity and countless games of charades, cards, and a number of other made-up activities, there is finally a knock at the door. Jumping at the sound, Sam answers it eagerly and finds a girl close to her own age standing there.

"Butterfingers sent me. You can go get your dinner now," she says quietly, looking past Sam and into the cabin with curiosity.

"Thank you!" Ally answers happily, already pulling her tennis shoes on. Before they have a chance to say anything further, the girl spins around and jogs back up the trail. She was probably instructed not to talk to them.

They've been in isolation for seven hours and they're both impatient to go the short distance to the lodge, to be back around other people. As they step into the kitchen however, it's apparent that Cowboy isn't pleased.

"So, as if the freezer running out of refrigerant weren't bad enough, you're telling me that my staff doesn't know how to do basic math and convert the recipes adequately?" Cowboy is lecturing a younger man, who is doing his best to look anywhere *but* at his boss.

Hearing the door close behind the girls, Cowboy looks up abruptly. "Sam," he says with some annoyance. "If you're here for dinner, you're too late. You and twenty other campers don't get a full meal tonight, thanks to our poor planning. Take what you want of what's left," he adds a bit more gently, gesturing to the back counter.

Sam sees some rice, rolls, and green beans that remain in the trays brought from the buffet table. Not wanting to get into the middle of the kitchen discussion, Sam and Ally grab a couple of plates and quickly fill them up. Mumbling thank you, they hurry outside.

Keeping to the shadows behind the lodge, they head back towards the trail, trying to avoid running into anyone. They haven't quite turned the corner, when a commotion from over near the bathrooms draws their attention.

"Eewww!" someone is saying loudly. "Why would anyone plug all the toilets up on *purpose*?" There's a large crowd gathered outside, and they're all talking excitedly to each other.

"I don't know," another girl answers, "but there's been a lot of stupid stuff happening. My friend came here earlier this summer and said the same thing. It's not as fun as it used to be. I don't think I'm going to come back next year."

Ms. Cooper strides angrily into the middle of the group then, on her way to the bathrooms with a plunger, effectively breaking up the crowd.

Sam and Ally jog as fast as they can back to the isolation cabin, managing not to spill all of their food. Once inside, they sit down at the table, relieved to have made it without incident.

"I'm beginning to understand why the camp is losing money," Ally says matter-of-factly, eating her cold rice.

"It's too bad," Sam replies. Poking at the congealed butter on the green beans, her appetite has faded. "Lexie and a lot of the other regulars would be really sad if it closed down."

"Maybe we should just let the whole raccoon thing go," Ally says softly. "You know…not make things any worse. If it *was* Sandy, I'm sure she already feels bad."

"I was thinking the same thing," Sam says without hesitation. "We'll be gone all day tomorrow for the creek walk and then two days for the horseback ride. Who cares about crabby Ms. Cooper anyway, right? *We* know the truth, and we've made some great friends. I think that's what Mr. Pine wanted Whispering Pines to be about: finding good friends."

Smiling again, Sam and Ally finish their food, determined to make the best of things. "What about Bigfoot?" Ally adds as an afterthought, pushing her empty plate away.

"Well…*that's* different," Sam says mischievously.

12

CREEK WALKING

Hours later, Sam is tucked away in bed, back at Cabin Navaho. The rest of the night passed surprisingly fast, although they were still relieved when Lexie came to get them.

Becky was the first to break the awkward silence after they returned, excited to tell them that she had passed the swim test. Her happiness was contagious, and by the time they all climbed into bed, the only thing on their minds was the daylong hike they were leaving for in the morning.

Butterfingers' light, rhythmic snoring is just loud enough to keep Sam awake. She's considering whether to throw a pillow at her when someone whispers her name.

"*Sam.*" There it is again. Turning over onto her stomach, Sam looks out into the dark room. She knows it isn't coming from beneath her.

"*Who is it?*" she whispers back, still searching the shadows for movement.

"It's me, dummy," Lexie says in a more normal voice, waving her hands out in front of her. Both of them are on the top bunks, so that their heads are only a few feet apart. Now that Sam's eyes have adjusted and she knows where to look, she can easily see the outline of her friend.

"Oh!" Sam answers, waving back. "What's up?"

Butterfingers' snoring pauses at the louder voices, but then continues, reassuring them that she's still asleep.

"I have something for you," Lexie says mysteriously, holding out her hand. Sam reaches across the gap and is surprised when she feels something hairy.

Pulling the item back, she studies it as best she can in the dark. It's two inches square, with course hair on one side and a smooth, solid backing on the other. "What in the world *is* this?" she asks, thoroughly confused.

"Before I went to get you at the cabin tonight, I took a little detour and went back to where you dropped the bark," Lexie confesses, lowering her voice again.

"You did *what?*" Sam gasps. "In the dark? Are you crazy?"

"Maybe...a little," Lexie laughs quietly. "It's not that far from the isolation cabin. It only took me ten minutes. Anyway," she continues, "when I was searching around the fallen log with my flashlight for the piece you dropped, I found *that* stuck on a broken branch."

It takes a minute for the implication to dawn on Sam, but when it does, she drops the hairy thing in disgust. "Oh my gosh! Is that a piece of Bigfoot's *skin?*" Noticing that she's let it fall onto her pillow, Sam quickly picks it back up gingerly with the very tips of her fingers. "That's *gross!*"

"Calm down," Lexie urges. "If you were looking at that in the light, you'd understand why I don't think it has anything to do with Bigfoot."

"What do you mean?" Sam asks, more

curious now than repulsed.

"The skin is cured, Sam. Like a pelt. I think it's probably from something made out of deer skin."

Sam is a little embarrassed now, realizing that the skin side is definitely too soft and pliable to be fresh. It reminds her of the little purses and shoes at gift shops made of rabbit or deer.

"Wait," she says with a jolt. "This means that whatever was out there was *wearing* something made out of deer skin?"

"Yup!" Lexie confirms, and Sam can see her silhouette nodding enthusiastically. "Sam, I think that someone is *pretending* to be Bigfoot!"

"But why would anyone do that?" Thoroughly confused now, Sam taps thoughtfully at her chin. "Do you think we should tell someone?"

"Tell them what?" Lexie counters. "Normally, being just a few feet outside the boundary wouldn't be a big deal, but with as much trouble as you've been in already…no. I don't think we should say anything. Besides, I think that whoever is doing this would *love* it if we told everyone. So let's not give him what he wants. Okay?"

Running her fingers over the deer hide, Sam considers their options. Lexie might be right. The most likely thing to happen is that they'd get in trouble for going where they shouldn't have. She and Ally could even be sent home. Then the Bigfoot rumors would just spread even more, hurting the camp's already suffering reputation. It's probably best to keep this to themselves.

"Okay," Sam finally agrees. "We won't say anything about this." Reaching out, she tries to give the clue back to Lexie.

"No, keep it," she insists. "You're more interested in it than I am."

Sam tucks it away under her pillow. As her eyes finally close and she drifts off to sleep, she's certain her dreams will be full of large, hairy creatures chasing her through the woods.

***

Sam doesn't have a chance to show the clue to Ally until later the next morning. While she doesn't remember dreaming about Bigfoot, she *did* dream about being lost in the woods, reinforcing a fear of the thick woods surrounding them now. Trying to shed the remnants of the nightmare, she walks alongside her best friend.

Pulling the small patch of skin and hair from her back pocket, she hands it to Ally. In hushed tones, she tells her what it is. They've been hiking for over an hour already, and they're all spread out along the trail. No one else can overhear them.

Shocked, but also excited by the mystery, Ally gives it back after studying it closely. "I agree, we can't tell anyone right now," she says, nodding. "They probably wouldn't even believe us. But what can we do about it?"

Shrugging, Sam stuffs it back in her pocket. "For now, just keep an eye out for other clues. Lexie and I talked more this morning. She's going to let Sandy and Becky in on it, so all of us will be looking."

"Do you think it's smart to tell Sandy?" Ally questions, looking back down the trail to where Lexie and Becky are walking together.

"Well, she was out there too, and Sandy doesn't seem like the type that would tell on herself."

Grinning, Ally can't argue with such a valid point. Squinting against the bright sunshine beating down on them, they fall silent again while concentrating on the uphill terrain.

As the day progresses, the long line of hikers tread deep into the Cascade Mountains. Sam has never been this far into these woods. The changing scenery is so grand that it's hard to compare it to anything else.

Just before lunchtime, the path suddenly drops over a ridge and down into a sharp ravine. As they carefully make the descent, Sam gazes at the distant tree line above them, and notices a large area of dead or dying trees. She points it out to Lexie, who doesn't seem too bothered by it.

"Probably beetles or something," Lexie suggests. "They can cause all sorts of problems."

When they finally reach the bottom of the ravine, a cool mountain creek greets them. Everyone is eager to get wet.

"Well come on!" their guide shouts, laughing. "This is why this activity is called 'creek walking.' Jump in!"

Laughing, the Cabin Navaho members are the first to splash into the clear, shallow water.

After the remaining fifty or so girls follow, the group continues along the creek, the part of the hike that gave the activity its name.

After more than an hour of a challenging course of slippery rocks, fallen trees and even a couple of small waterfalls, they finally reach their destination. Coming around a particularly sharp bend, Sam stops abruptly, causing Ally and Becky to crash into her.

"Isn't it amazing?" Lexie shouts, splashing ahead of them.

Looming before them is the opening to a massive cave. Huge boulders as large as cars are scattered around its entrance, making it appear even more surreal. Sam feels like an ant in comparison, and cranes her neck to look up at the caverns' ceiling once inside.

It's like being in another world. Long daggers of rock reach down towards them, almost met by identical formations rising up from the ground.

"These formations are called stalactites and stalagmites," their guide explains, running his hand over their odd, lumpy surfaces. "The stalactites are the ones that look like icicles on the ceiling. They're formed over thousands of years by water dripping. The mineral in that water then creates the stalagmites that build up underneath."

Completely enthralled by the odd creations, Sam barely acknowledges the sack lunch that's handed to her. She's seen pictures of these in books before and on some travel show years ago, but this is the first time in person. Digging the flashlight out of her backpack, she explores a bit farther into the unique cave.

The creek they were walking in flows through a section of the cave, meandering around the large rocks and stalagmites. Sam carefully picks her way through it, following the somewhat sparkly and mesmerizing rocks.

"Sam!" Ally calls out, trying to keep up. "Don't go too far. I don't like being this far in."

Pausing, Sam climbs up onto a nearby boulder with a flattened top, and Ally joins her. The light from the entrance just barely reaches them, but it's enough that they can see without the flashlights on. Taking out their sandwiches, they hungrily start eating while listening to all of the girls making various echoes in other parts of the cave.

Sam gets halfway through her food, when suddenly a horrible stench reaches her. "Ugh!" she gags. "What's that *smell?*" Grabbing the flashlight again, she slips down on the opposite side and starts looking around. It doesn't take long to follow the disgusting odor back to its source.

Piled up in a large crevasse on the underside of the rock are more than a dozen dead trout, carried there by the water. A little relieved to discover it isn't something worse, Sam starts to turn away when something else catches her attention.

Floating past the rotting fish is some sort of multi-colored piece of paper. Intrigued, Sam leans over and snatches it before it can disappear. Squinting, she studies the faded wording. *Mountain Construction, LLC.* Figuring it must be some sort of label, she folds it carefully, placing it in her pocket with the tuft of hair.

The hoots and groans bouncing off the walls echo the thoughts tumbling around in her head. Somehow, she knows these items are connected, and she's determined to find out how.

13

SANDY

They make it back to camp just before dinnertime and go directly to the lodge to eat. Once gathered at their table, Sam realizes that Sandy isn't there. Spotting Butterfingers, she flags her down.

"Do you know where Sandy is?" she asks. "Have they gotten back from the kayaking trip yet?"

"They got back an hour ago," Butterfingers explains. "But Sandy had an…exciting afternoon and went to lie down." Before Sam can get any more information, their counselor walks away, leaving them all guessing.

"Let's hurry up and finish eating," Becky urges. "I want to make sure she's okay."

"Do you think we should have told her about our, umm…discovery?" Ally worries. "Maybe she blabbed about it to someone and got in trouble."

Lexie pauses with a spoonful of pork and beans halfway to her mouth, concerned. Looking around as if expecting Ms. Cooper to come marching up to them, she swallows hard. "She better not have, or else she'll find worse than a raccoon in her bed!"

So Lexie thinks Sandy was responsible for the raccoon incident too, Sam considers. Rushing to finish her cheeseburger, she hopes they'll still get to leave for the overnight horseback ride in the morning. It was the one thing she'd been looking forward to the most.

By the time the four of them burst into the cabin, they all have various ideas of what they're going to find and how they're going to handle it. However, the reality comes as a shock. Sandy is curled up on her bed, sound asleep. Her normally well-kept hair is in disarray, splayed out around her head, damp and knotted. Her tennis shoes are scattered on the floor, sopping wet. It's clear her backpack took a dunking, too.

Sam is surprised, since Sandy had been bragging about how good she is at kayaking. She even claimed to own one and to use it regularly at a lake near her home. The group was being bussed to a large lake not too far away, so it wasn't swift water. How could she have rolled it?

"Sandy?" she asks hesitantly. "Are you awake?"

Opening her eyes, Sandy rubs them and then sits up slowly. "You're back," is all she says.

"What happened?" Becky demands. She sits down on the bed next to her friend, and puts a supportive arm around her damp shoulders.

"I'm fine," Sandy insists. "But I'm *never* coming back to this stupid camp! They have wild animals in our cabins, untrained staff, stopped-up toilets, not enough food, and worn-out equipment. My kayak had a *hole* in it! Can you believe that? I got nearly halfway out on the lake before I realized that the water in the bottom of it was more than normal. By the time I got turned around and headed back, it was quickly getting worse." Turning now to face them all, she's near tears.

"I was faster than everyone else there, so I was way out ahead. I was told not to go so far, but I ignored them. So when the kayak sunk, I was still a good distance away from the group. I had a life vest on, of course, but all of my stuff was stowed in the kayak. We were rowing over to the other side and then going on a hike before having lunch. So I had my backpack with all of my stuff in it. I had to float on my back and try to hold my bag up for ten minutes before someone heard me yelling for help and finally spotted me.

"All of the kayaks were one-person, so I had to hold onto a rope and get towed by the guide. It was cold and humiliating. I just want to go home!"

"Did you talk to anyone about going home?" Becky asks, sounding worried. "We all want you to stay and go on the horseback ride with us tomorrow! Right, you guys?" she asks, looking to Sam, Ally, and Lexie.

"Of course we do!"

Lexie is quick to answer, surprising Sam, who can't help but wonder if Lexie's enthusiasm is genuine, or if she is thinking more about protecting the camp. Sandy's father *was* trying to buy it, and if he were to find out just how much the camp is struggling, it might give him some leverage with the board.

"Stop it you guys," Sandy says harshly. "None of you actually like me, you're just pretending. It's okay. I'm used to it. No one ever *really* wants to be my friend…not even my parents. They're more concerned with how our family appears to everyone else instead."

Sam and Ally sit on the other side of Sandy, crowding onto the lower bunk. Gathered around their unexpected friend, Sam feels guilty for being so judgmental of her from the beginning. She can't imagine how horrible it would be to feel that way.

"I like you, Sandy," she says honestly. "We might not have a lot in common, but you're fun to be around, once someone gets to know you."

"Yeah, and you're funny, too!" Ally adds.

"And brave," Becky says softly. "I wish I were as brave as you are, Sandy. You aren't afraid to do anything, or to tell people exactly what's on your mind. I could never do that. I think I would have had a heart attack if I had been stuck out in the middle of a lake!"

"They're right," Lexie admits, somewhat reluctantly. "I know that I've given you a hard time, but I think it might be because I was jealous. I thought you had the perfect life, and parents that were actually there for you."

Sam is stunned at the confession, and she can see the immediate effect that it has. Sandy's features soften, and she seems to finally give in and accept the friendship that's being offered.

"I don't think I've ever had real girlfriends before," she confesses, wiping absently at a lone tear.

"Well, now you have four!" Lexie tells her, kneeling down in front of the group on the bed. "And friends look out for each other, right?" she asks, looking at each of them.

"Right!" they all answer, bound together by something none of them could put into words.

14

TRAIL OF DANGER

The sun is hot on their backs as they settle into the saddles and prepare to start out on the much anticipated trail ride.

Somehow, Sam ended up on the first horse, a large mare with white and black patches, named Sundance. They were already off to a rocky start, with Sam struggling to keep her mount from trying to eat every leafy thing in reach.

Sam was delighted to discover that Cowboy is part of the trail team, which explains his nickname. There are twenty girls on the overnight trip and that means a whole lot of horses to manage, so there are two other handlers, as well as two counselors. Butterfingers had to stay back at camp to help Ms. Cooper with various tasks. The girls have strict instructions to be on their best behavior.

Despite Cowboy's obvious knowledge, he isn't in charge. As soon as the girls had arrived early this morning, a young man named Zorro had started barking out orders. In his twenties, he's well over six feet tall and pushing two-hundred and fifty pounds. His attitude matches his tough physique.

Where Cowboy is laid back and in control, the third man is just the opposite. Ranger seems eager to please Zorro and practically trips over his own feet while running to do everything he demands. Also in his twenties, he's skinny and not quite as tall as Zorro. Sam recognizes him as the same guy that Cowboy was criticizing for messing up dinner the other night.

Zorro is leading the ride on a massive black horse in front of Sam. He cautioned her to stay a good distance behind him, as his steed doesn't like to be crowded.

Cowboy is the middle of the pack, with

Ranger taking up the rear. The riders have been grouped first according to their cabin, then by riding ability. Sam had the most experience, so was given the biggest responsibility.

"Sundance is a pig," Ally laughs. She has to pull up short again while Sam fights to gain control.

"Do you want to trade?" Sam turns around in her saddle once she has her horse back on the trail. She looks longingly at Ally's calm, chestnut colored mount. "Or anyone?" she says more loudly to Lexie, Becky and Sandy.

The three other girls are directly behind them. Grinning, they all shake their heads vigorously. "I should have warned you," Lexie chuckles. "I got her once last year. She's nice and all, just....very hungry."

Facing forward again, Sam lets out a big sigh and gathers up the reins a bit tighter. They have five hours of riding ahead of them. It took close to an hour to hike up to the starting point, so it'll be a late lunch once they arrive at the temporary camp that's already set up.

Honestly, even though the horse is a pain, she doesn't mind. Just being in the saddle, riding through the woods, is a dream come true. Closing her eyes, Sam tilts her head up to the sun and lets it wash over her, much the same way it's cleansing the mountains. There was a thick layer of mist on the trail when they first started out. But it's already lifting and blowing away in the light, warm breeze scented with pine. Mixed in now with the smell of the woods is saddle soap, leather, and the distinct aroma of horse that still lingers in the old barn at Sam's house.

The reins in Sam's hands go taught, jerking her out of her trance. "Ugh!" she groans, fighting once again with her new, stubborn friend who's found some large, green leafy plant that just *has* to be eaten.

"Get that horse under control!" Zorro yells from up ahead. "I don't want to see her off the trail."

"Geez, maybe they should put that horse at the back, instead of the front," Becky mutters.

"I said the same thing when I had her," Lexie agrees. "But Cowboy explained that she's old and stubborn and the only way she'll do the trail is if she's leading. That's another reason Zorro is staying so far out."

"Humph. Leave the stupid horse in the barn, then," Sandy complains. Her own ride is a beautiful white mare with a long, flowing mane. She had rushed to claim her as soon as spotting her this morning.

"Nah…Sundance is an icon here," Lexie tells them. "She was one of the first horses ever used on the trail ride and was Mr. Pine's own horse. According to Cowboy, it was even written into his will that she be taken care of after his passing."

Knowing this, Sam sits a little taller in the saddle and pats at Sundance's long, sturdy neck. "Well, we're going to be friends. Right, old girl?" she says happily. Snickering, the horse tosses her head and then promptly goes for a patch of long grass.

The morning stretches on, but they travel the trail much faster than the day before and they soon find themselves at the top of the same, steep ravine as yesterday. Although they're farther up from where they had climbed down, it's still in the same general location.

Actually, Sam thinks to herself, *we're in the clump of dead trees that I saw!* Looking around with more interest, Sam notes that it's a small area of brown at the top of the cliff. However, it follows a group of sparse trees all the way down to the water at the bottom, making an odd line of death.

Zorro turns to the left, taking the well-trampled trail upstream, in the opposite direction of the creek walk. Following him at a distance, Sam looks nervously to her right. Although they're a good two feet from the drop-off, being up on the horse makes her feel like she's about to fall over the side.

Her friends just make the turn behind her, when suddenly Sundance decides to go her own way again. But *this* time, it isn't for a snack. With growing horror, Sam pulls desperately at the reins as she realizes that she's heading straight for the edge!

15

THE MASK OF ZORRO

Crying out in alarm as Sundance sidesteps from her yanking, Sam is sure they're both about to plummet to their deaths. But as Ally starts to scream a warning behind her, Sam sees there's a narrow deer trail that her horse is trying to follow.

"Whoa, there!" Cowboy yells. Sam can hear the sound of heavy hoof beats pounding towards her.

Still struggling to get control, Sam is less fearful now that she knows the ground doesn't actually fall away. Leaning back in the saddle to give Sundance more leverage, she tries to guide her back onto the main trail. Neighing loudly in protest and tossing her head wildly, Sundance finally backs up a couple of steps, bucks slightly, and then lunges forward, straight for Zorro!

Relieved to be back on solid ground, Sam continues to scramble in the saddle, now trying to shift her weight forward. Digging in her knees, she leans down close to the spooked horse's neck. "Whoa girl," she says firmly, while pulling down on the reins and trying to turn her in a circle to the left. This was a technique she had learned a couple of years ago, a good way to stop a runaway horse.

Fortunately, it works. She manages to stop Sundance a few feet from the testy, black stallion. Apparently, it isn't enough, because the stallion reacts violently and it takes Zorro several minutes to calm him down.

Meanwhile, Cowboy has come up alongside Sam. The rest of the riders are all lined up on the trail behind them, crowded together, trying to get a glimpse of the commotion. "What's going on up there?" Ranger demands, trapped at the back of the pack.

"I'll tell you what's going on!" Zorro

bellows, jumping down to the ground. Stomping towards Sam, he points a large finger at her. "The problem is that we've got someone who doesn't know how to ride safely. Get off that horse!" he demands, his anger apparent.

Sam once again finds herself at the other end of an unfair accusation. But this time, she is too intimidated by the furious man to even think of arguing back. Doing her best not to burst into tears, she silently slides from the saddle.

"You can walk that horse from here on, since you obviously can't ride it!" Zorro declares, still wagging a finger at her.

"Now wait just a minute!" Cowboy intervenes. "You can hardly blame the girl. Last time I checked, this was a camp for young ladies. We shouldn't be putting them on a horse that can't stay on the trail!"

"That's why you don't give the horse its own lead!" Zorro argues, his voice getting even louder. "She had to have let up on the reins. I told her specifically to keep 'em tight. And last time I checked, old man, my name was the one on the side of the horse trailer, *not* yours! If I want your opinion, I'll ask for it."

His face turning a dark crimson, Cowboy dismounts smoothly from his own horse and hands the reins to Sam. Taking a somewhat menacing step towards Zorro, he veers off towards the woods and motions curtly for the younger man to follow him.

Sam looks at Ally and sees her own dismay mirrored on her friend's face.

"Are you okay?" Ally asks, swallowing hard. "I thought for sure that you were going to fall!"

"I'm fine," Sam manages to croak out. Standing somewhat awkwardly, holding the reins for both horses, she looks behind Ally to Lexie. "What is *that* all about?" she asks, angling her chin towards the two men arguing now in hushed tones.

"Cowboy's been here forever," Lexie explains, "but Zorro was put in charge of the horses this year. I don't know the details, but it was obvious at the last camp session that they don't get along."

"Well, the guy's a jerk," Sandy whispers. "That wasn't your fault, Sam. He's probably just afraid your parents will sue him if he doesn't act like you did something wrong."

"Hey, what's the hold up?" Ranger has gotten tired of waiting and brought his horse up.

"Nothing, get back to your post," Cowboy barks, walking briskly back to the waiting girls. His face is still red, and now Zorro's is, too. Without another word, the younger man gets on his horse and starts riding back up the trail.

"Here, you'll be on Lucky from now on," Cowboy tells Sam, taking Sundance's reins from her. "I think it best if we just switch. He's a bit uppity, but a smart horse. Can you ride behind Becky back there and keep an eye on the other girls?"

Sam is so relieved that she could hug him, but doesn't want to make an even bigger scene. She'd pay anything to know what he said to Zorro. "Thank you," she simply says instead.

"Nothing to thank me for." Winking once, Cowboy expertly swings up into the saddle and starts them on their way again.

A little nervous to get back on a horse, Sam is happy to find that Lucky is very mellow and falls into his rightful place without her even having to guide him.

Fortunately, the rest of the afternoon goes without incident. By the time they reach their overnight camp, Sam has finally relaxed and is enjoying herself again. As the horses all gather in an open field next to the tents to graze, they begin to dismount and help get the saddles off.

Doing their best to avoid Zorro, Sam and Ally carry their tack over to some logs, where they were instructed to lay it all out. Draping the damp horse blanket, Sam studies some of the other gear that's spread out, and pauses. Set on top of the log that's next to theirs, are the tan saddlebags that Sam had spent a couple of hours staring at today. Zorro's bags. Now that she sees them up close, it's clear that they're made out of deer hide.

"Ally," she says, the excitement in her voice clear.

Curious, Ally finishes arranging her things and then steps up next to Sam. "What is it?" she asks, turning to look at what Sam is pointing at. It takes her a minute, but then she makes the connection. "The hair in the woods," she concludes. "But Sam, there's a lot of things made out of deer hide. That doesn't mean it's him."

Sam startles Ally by taking her by the shoulders and pulling her down. They're now both squatting next to the horse blanket at eye-level, with the bag a few feet away. "Even if it's missing a piece the same size as the one we found?" she asks smugly.

Ally can now see that there is, in fact, a hole in one of the bags…and she's guessing that their clue would fit in it perfectly!

***

"Why would Zorro be sneaking around in the woods, pretending to be Bigfoot?" Becky wants to know.

The sun set over an hour ago, and they've all gathered around a large fire to roast marshmallows before bed. It's the first opportunity they've had to talk about their most recent discovery. Sitting as far off to one side as possible without drawing any criticism, the five of them huddle together and speak in hushed tones.

"I don't know much about Zorro," Lexie admits. "Except that his dad owns the horse outfit and he seems pretty close to Ms. Cooper. Cowboy sure doesn't like him, but you don't need *me* to tell you that."

"Maybe we should tell Cowboy?" Ally suggests, always the prudent one.

Sam considers this carefully. If Cowboy believed them, then what? He would have to talk with Ms. Cooper when they got back, which would lead to more of her wrath. Or...he wouldn't believe them, in which case, they would be in for an even *bigger* dose of Ms. Cooper's discipline.

"No," Sam replies, shaking her head. "We don't really have anything to tell him, except that we *might* have proof that he was in the same area where we saw something big that made a weird sound. A place that was supposed to be off-limits. Zorro would probably come up with some sort of explanation and we'd be blamed for having wild imaginations."

"Maybe that's all it is." The voice of reason belongs to Sandy, who grins in response to their shocked expressions. "I'm just saying that we really don't know w*hat* we saw, and I agree with Sam; we'd sound pretty stupid accusing

Zorro of it."

Having it put that way, Sam feels kind of silly now. They all decide to keep it to themselves and then join the rest of the campers for the last song.

There are three large canvas tents in the clearing, with the girls and counselors in two of them and the three men in the third. As the campfire dies down, darkness spills in from the woods. Soon the silence is complete, interrupted occasionally by a horse's snicker or whinny.

Lying in her sleeping bag, Sam is sure that she's the only one still awake. The heavy, rhythmic breathing of sleeping campers surrounds her and she longs to join them. However, she can't seem to shut her brain off and instead replays the scene from earlier over and over again. Although certain she didn't do anything wrong, she can't help but wonder if she *should* have kept a tighter grip on the reins, or if maybe she was distracted by the dead trees.

A cracking branch near the tent draws her attention, and she is instantly wide awake. Holding her breath, she strains to hear other noises. She is rewarded by the distinct sound of carefully placed footsteps leading away from the tents, towards the horses. The makeshift bathroom is in the other direction, so Sam is immediately suspicious.

Not wanting to wake anyone, she crawls quietly from her bedding and peeks her head through the opening. Unable to make out anything in the thick darkness, she slips out of the tent and creeps in the direction of the sound, her bare feet silent in the pine needles.

She doesn't have far to go before she hears a whispered conversation on the light breeze. More curious now than scared, she tiptoes towards it, ducking behind a large tree when two men's dark forms come into view.

"I told you before to take that horse out of the line-up!" The voice belongs to Zorro, and Ranger answers him.

"She's the only one willing to walk that trail in the dark, man. You know that! I don't care what the old man's will says...you can't have it both ways. She does one or the other, but not both."

Sam peeks out cautiously when there's a pause in the dialogue.

"We'll figure it out later, but Cowboy's starting to ask questions," Zorro responds. He hands something to Ranger then, slapping it into his palm. "Here's your share. You've got twelve barrels for me to take back tomorrow night, correct?"

"Umm…yeah. About that," Ranger says uneasily, shoving the package into his jacket pocket. "I got eleven to go back. I, ah…I lost one."

"You lost *another* one?" Zorro says menacingly. "I told you before, that's not acceptable! You're going to come back here tomorrow and find it. We can't be leaving that kind of evidence behind. Especially not now!"

"Come on, man!" Ranger whines. "There ain't nobody out here but us. You're starting to get paranoid, and I *hate* climbing down to the bottom."

"Then you shouldn't have dropped it. And I don't pay you to *think*. I'm the one taking the risks. You just do what I tell you, and it'll work out fine. Now…I'll be at the trailhead tomorrow night at midnight for the pickup. I want all twelve empties. Got it?"

"Sure, man. Sure." Ranger concedes. Backing away from the much larger man, he holds his hands out in surrender. "Whatever you say."

Shrinking into the shadows, Sam holds her breath and watches as the two conspirators walk back past her. *There's a lot more going on here than just scaring some girls at a camp,* Sam realizes with a start. Her heart is hammering so loud that she's sure they'll hear her.

After several minutes pass without her being discovered, she silently makes her way back to the tent and climbs into her safe, warm sleeping bag. Afraid of making any noise, she decides to wait until morning to tell the other girls about it. With thoughts of Bigfoot, dead trees, and Ms. Cooper's accusing eyes swirling through her head, she finally falls asleep.

16

SABOTAGED!

Ally and Becky are horrified to learn that Sam has snuck around in the dark woods by herself, but both Sandy and Lexie are impressed.

"Just wake me up next time!" Lexie begs as they gather their stuff together for the ride back to camp.

"Shhh," Becky cautions, looking around to make sure no one is eavesdropping. "What do you think it means?"

"It means that these creeps are doing something illegal out here. This camp is getting even weirder," Sandy says bluntly. Pulling her hair up into a ponytail, she focuses on Sam. "Too bad you've got everyone so mad at us. And it's still your word against his."

Biting at her lip, Sam can't come up with a valid argument. Sandy's right again. Sam isn't even put off by her directness. She's used to it now, and understands that it isn't personal, but just the way Sandy is.

"So we just need to figure the rest of this out in the next two days," Sam finally concludes.

"Right," Ally agrees. "We all should be on the lookout for anything odd or out of place."

Cowboy hollers for everybody to mount up, so the discussion ends. He had guided Sam towards Lucky without comment when they started gearing up the horses, so he is now at the front on Sundance.

Ranger is staying behind at the camp with the three horses used to pack in all of the food and water. Zorro replaces him at the end of the line, his testy stallion nipping at a couple of horses on the way.

The rhythm of the swaying horses is hypnotic. When they all come to a stop, it seems like minutes have passed instead of hours, Looking up in surprise, Sam discovers that they are already back at the trailhead. Of course, the lack of sleep she had the night before might have something to do with her lack of attention to time, as well.

A rough gravel road leads away into the woods and a large truck and horse trailer are parked on it. It was also there the day before, and Sam assumes that it's how they move the horses in and out. A good sized pasture's been fenced off, and there are a couple of small buildings for storage. This must enable them to keep the horses there for a day or two, in between the rides.

"I don't think my rear end has ever been this sore," Sandy moans, sliding down painfully to the ground. "But it was still fun," she quickly adds, smiling at Becky.

After another sack lunch, it's already mid-afternoon. The girls say goodbye to the horses and hike down to the main trail. Sam and Ally are relieved to leave Zorro behind to finish tending to the animals.

The young counselors lead them in marching songs, and the next hour is a great reminder of how much fun Camp Whispering

Pines really is. Ally finds a perfectly shaped, weathered stick for the mast on their barge, which launches a treasure hunt by all twenty girls. Several unique items are spotted right along the trail. Each time the finders are convinced it will make theirs the winning boat.

By the time they get back to Cabin Navaho, their soreness is almost forgotten and the girls are ready for another fun night.

"I can't believe that tomorrow is Thursday already. We've only got one full day left," Becky remarks. "I'm sure going to miss all of you."

Ally notes how much stronger Becky's voice is. She certainly doesn't seem like the same shy, timid girl they met just a few days ago.

"You know, it's funny," Sandy replies. "I thought my parents were trying to get rid of me again by sending me here. But I guess they might have been right about this being a good experience, because I'm going to miss you, too!"

Lexie is being unusually quiet, and Sam looks at her questioningly. "Lexie," she says softly, getting the other girls attention. "What did you mean the other day, when you said you were jealous of Sandy?"

Shuffling her feet, Lexie looks back at Sam briefly before staring at the floor. "A couple of years ago, my older brother was killed in a car accident. My parents were so busy grieving, that they forgot they still had a daughter." Although her voice is steady, she dabs at her eyes. "I got used to taking care of myself. That's when I started spending my summers here. But now," she continues, her voice hardening, "I might lose this place, too. My folks have been trying to get me to stay home and spend time with them again, so they'll use all this stuff as an excuse to say I can't come anymore. Or else it'll be shut down altogether." Throwing her backpack up on the bed, she turns away from the worried stares of her friends.

"Maybe that wouldn't be such a bad thing." Ally suggests. When Lexie turns and looks at her sharply, she's quick to explain herself. "I mean, spending time with your mom and dad. Maybe you can talk to them, Lexie, and agree to just not come as often. Let them know how important the camp is to you, but don't you think you should give them a chance, too? I'm sure they must love you."

"I wish *my* parents wanted to spend more time with me," Sandy says. "But no matter what, I think that all of us should write down our emails and phone numbers, so that we can stay in contact after camp. You *do* have phones or computers, right?"

Lexie smiles, nodding enthusiastically. Taking her backpack down again, she digs around and finally produces a notebook and pen. "Here!" she directs, handing it to Sandy. "You start. Everyone jot down your info and I'll make copies of it for all of us!"

Sam's just finished adding her phone number when Butterfingers barges into the cabin, startling them all. Without even acknowledging the other girls, she turns to Ally and Sam. "I need to talk with you," she says bluntly.

"Okay…" Sam says, setting the paper aside. "What's up?"

"Just come with me." Spinning around, she leaves as abruptly as she entered.

"This can't be good," Ally moans, getting slowly to her feet.

By the time they step outside, Butterfingers has already started walking away from the cabin and the two girls hurry after her. "What now?" Sam asks, getting more anxious.

Approaching the bottom of the trail where it branches off to the lodge and other buildings, she turns on them. They're both shocked by the obvious anger on their counselor's normally friendly face.

"I don't have anything to say to you, but Ms. Cooper does. She's waiting for you in her office."

Before they can even ask questions, Butterfingers marches away from them, her hands balled into fists at her sides.

"Oh geez," Sam breathes, looking fearfully towards the director's office. "Why does this keep happening to us?" Reaching out to take Ally's hand for comfort, the two of them inch closer.

Before they're clear of the tree line, the big red truck with the horse trailer comes roaring up and stops right in front of their destination. Sam remembers seeing a dirt road over on the far side of the clearing. Evidently, this must be one that leads to where the horses are kept.

Zorro climbs down from the pickup and

leaps up the front steps. "Aunt Cooper, are you in there?" he hollers, pulling at the door without waiting for an answer.

Sam and Ally look at each other, dumbfounded. "Aunt?" they both whisper at the same time. Turning back to the truck, Sam notices the sign on the side of it for the first time.

Mountain Construction, LLC.

Family Owned and Operated Business.

Mark and Steven Pine.

Pulling out the weathered label she found in the cave from her pocket, Sam holds it out to Ally. The colorful logo in the background is an exact match. *But what is Zorro doing here now?* Sam worries. Something tells her that it has everything to do with her near trip down the ravine.

It takes all of their combined courage to enter the small building, but they do it together and find Zorro behind the desk with Ms. Cooper. They appear to be in the middle of a serious discussion, but stop abruptly when they spot the girls..

"Sam, Ally. I'm going to make this short, because I don't like playing games." If Sam had thought Ms. Cooper sounded harsh before, that was nothing compared to her tone now. "I've already spoken with your parents. You're being expelled from Camp Whispering Pines. They will be here tomorrow to pick you up."

Staring at her in stunned silence, both girls are at a loss for words. Sam's heart feels like it fell into her stomach, and she's afraid that she might throw up. Looking at Ally's pale complexion, she's guessing her best friend is feeling the same.

"But...I-I don't understand," Sam practically wails. "What did we do wrong?"

"I *told* you that I don't play games!" the older woman shouts, slamming a hand down onto her desk. "I looked into you," she continues, wagging a finger as Sam. "I had heard you might have an issue with authority. Was our camp not exciting enough for you girls, so that you had to drum up some of your own drama?"

"What in the *world* are you talking about?" Ally demands, impressing Sam with how steady she sounds. "You can at least tell us what we're being accused of."

"I don't have to explain myself to you, but for the record..." Ms. Cooper begins, pushing at a folder to lift a paper out from underneath it. As she does this, something small is shoved off the edge of the desk, and lands on the floor near Sam's feet. Happy for a distraction, she glances down at it and sees that it's a business card. All she can make out is the larger print in the middle: *Hollingsworth Industries.* Wasn't that Sandy's last name?

Clearing her throat, the director starts reading from an actual list. "Violating our pool safety policy by interfering with the rescue of a struggling swimmer. Violating our camp rules by storing food inside a cabin. Disrespecting the administration by arguing about said violations. Violating camp rules by going outside the marked boundaries." Zorro looks pointedly at Sam and she shifts uncomfortably in the chair.

"Then there's the incident on the trail ride." Miss Cooper continues, looking directly at Sam. "Another situation instigated by *not* following the directions that were clearly outlined for you. You jeopardized your safety, the life of the horse you were on *and* the other riders that could have followed you."

"How can you possibly blame-" Ally starts to argue, but Sam silences her by calmly placing a hand on her arm.

"It doesn't matter," Sam says softly. When Ms. Cooper and Zorro exchange a surprised look at her comment, she takes advantage of the distraction by putting her foot on top of the business card and slowly drawing it back towards her.

"Well, as if that wasn't enough already," Ms. Cooper insists, deciding to ignore Sam. "We had a camper come forward this afternoon and admit to seeing the two of you fleeing the bathrooms right before the vandalism was discovered the other night. While I might tolerate some of the other poor behaviors, *that* is something we simply cannot allow to go unpunished. That kind of criminal act spreads harmful rumors and sheds a very poor light on our organization. Camp Whispering Pines can't afford that sort of negative reputation."

Ally has begun to openly weep, but while Sam feels horrible, she is more convinced than ever about a growing suspicion. Pretending to also be upset, she places her head in her hands, and peeks between her fingers to confirm that the business card is now directly under her.

"Come on," Zorro says with contempt. "It's your own fault. Don't expect us to feel sorry for you."

"Don't worry," Sam replies coolly, raising her head to meet his gaze. "I would never ask for anything so…decent from you."

Reaching for a dazed Ally, Sam also makes a blind grab for the card under her shoe and palms it before standing. Pulling her friend after her, they stumble through the door as Ms. Cooper calls out behind them.

"Enjoy your final supper girls, and then get your stuff packed and tell your friends goodbye. You leave first thing in the morning!"

17

PIECES OF A PUZZLE

"This is crazy!" Ally says in disbelief. They make it as far as the bottom of the hill before she pulls at Sam until she stops. "Why didn't you defend us? Do you have *any* idea how mad our parents are going to be? We'll never hear the end of this!"

"Arguing with them wasn't going to do us any good," Sam answers. Her tone causes Ally to pause and study her friend more closely.

"Sam..." she begins, cautious. "I've seen that look on your face before. You've figured something out, haven't you?" Her excitement growing, Ally glances around to make sure no one else is nearby. "Come on, spill it!"

In response, Sam turns her left hand over, revealing the business card cupped in her palm. "Ms. Cooper knocked this off her desk," she explains. Able to examine it now, she confirms it's the standard business info on the front, and reads it aloud.

"Wait," Ally stops her. "Hollingsworth. Isn't that Sandy's last name?" Brows furrowed, she purses her lips. "Why would *she* have that?"

Sam flips the card over without answering, and discovers a handwritten message:

"It was a pleasure to meet with you and your brother. I hope to hear from you soon," Sam reads, squinting at the scribbled text. "There's a phone number, too. I'm guessing it's her father's personal cell."

"But I still don't get why you let her say all of those lies about us." Ally states, her arms crossed over her chest.

"Because she already *knows* they're lies, Ally," Sam says. "I'll explain what I mean, but I think we need to talk with Sandy first."

They find the three other girls still at Cabin Navaho. Thankfully, Butterfingers isn't there. Sam's confidence might be growing, but she's not sure she could convince their counselor yet.

Trying to collect her thoughts, Sam closes the screen door and then leans up against it. "You're going to want to sit down for this," she tells her friends, rubbing at her eyes. She can feel a headache coming on, but forces herself to talk. They're all dismayed when they find out what happened, and start asking several questions all at once.

"Wait!" Sam stops them, putting her hands up to ward off the interrogation. "There's more." She tells them about the matching logo on the truck and about Zorro calling Ms. Cooper his aunt. Finally, she hands Sandy the business card. "This was on her desk."

"This *is* my dad's," Sandy acknowledges. "And that's his handwriting. But why do you think it's so strange, Sam? I already told you that he was here. Ms. Cooper *is* the director, and remember, this place isn't even for sale, so there wasn't a real estate agent to show them around."

"If it wasn't for sale," Becky asks, "then how did he find it?"

"Daddy is a pro at digging up large corporations that are failing, and then bailing them out. Most of the time, it's mismanagement by the owners, so he's able to turn a big profit, even though that's not why he wants it. But I already told you that the board voted it down."

"We've been assuming that Ms. Cooper was *against* selling the camp," Sam mutters, pacing the floor. "But then why would your dad be looking forward to talking with her and Zorro's father? That suggests that she was his contact. What if Ms. Cooper was actually the one who *wanted* to sell? What if she was mad and not talking to her three sisters because they voted her and her brother down?" Pausing, Sam looks up to find four stunned faces staring at her revelation.

"But why?" Becky wants to know. "Why would she want to sell it?"

"That, we don't know," Lexie answers, when Sam shrugs in response. "But it would explain a lot."

"I'm still not really following you," Ally admits. "It might explain why she's in such a bad mood and not really caring that things aren't being kept up. But what does it have to do with us?"

"Think about it," Sam urges, turning to Ally. "Ms. Cooper said she had heard about us and 'looked into' me, so I'll bet she read the article about us solving the Hollow Inn mystery that ran in our local paper. I could tell from the beginning that she had it in for me. She knew that we'd be quick to poke around where we shouldn't."

"What mystery?" Becky asks, wide-eyed. Sam and Ally quickly explain their excitement from a few weeks before that had ended with a run-in with a gun-wielding transient.

"That's a cool story and all," Sandy replies with her typical attitude. "But it still has nothing to do with this camp."

"I think it does," Sam counters. "We were put into a cabin with the most loyal and well-known camper here, *and* the daughter of the man trying to buy it. What better way to spread the rumors and stories of all of the mishaps? Ms. Cooper thought she had a couple of perfect scapegoats. And I don't think it was a coincidence that Sandy's kayak sank. That alone might be enough for her dad to manipulate the board into selling."

"You could be right," Sandy agrees, standing up slowly with a new sense of purpose. "I was even falling for it. Remember after I got back from kayaking? I already had a list of troubles to share with my father. If he were to find out that I could have drowned due to faulty equipment, he could threaten to shut this place down. He'd have them begging him to buy!" Sandy puts a hand over her mouth while turning to look sheepishly at Lexie. "I'm sorry."

"It's okay, Sandy," Lexie mumbles, her normal energy drained. "This whole summer has been different, anyway. Things *do* need to change, but I just wish the camp could stay open, not get turned into a corporate retreat."

"What can we do about it?" Becky pleads, looking at each of them.

"I can talk to my dad after he picks me up on Friday," Sandy assures her. "I promise," she continues, looking at Lexie. "I'll explain everything to him. He'll know what to do!"

Doing her best to smile, Lexie thanks Sandy and then goes back to writing in her notebook, where she's copying all of their contact information down on separate sheets. "At least we'll be able to talk to each other, no matter what happens with the camp," she says, trying to stay positive.

"You guys still have all day tomorrow to have fun," Ally adds. "Don't worry about us. Sam and I have been in worse trouble."

"Do you have to go to the isolation cabin?" Lexie wants to know. When they shake their heads no, her smile broadens. "It stinks that you have to leave in the morning, but tonight is one of the best nights of the week. Trust me!"

Encouraged by her friend's enthusiasm, Sam begins to see the brighter side of things…but then she remembers that her mom will be coming for her tomorrow. In spite of what Ally said, Sam can't think of another time that she was ever accused of doing such things. She only wishes they could prove their innocence.

18

ANSWERS IN THE DARK

Sam was hoping to see Cowboy at dinner. She didn't know what she was going to say, but she wants him to know about her and Sam being sent home…and why. But he was nowhere to be seen. When she asked one of the food servers, they said he had to go into town to get some food. He'd be back either late that night or the next day.

Word of their expulsion traveled fast and they receive plenty of looks with whispered conversation. However, several girls come up to give Sam and Ally support. The young girl that

Sam helped in the pool approaches to tell them how sorry she is and that she doesn't think it's fair they're being sent home. As she walks away, Sam realizes why Ms. Cooper didn't put them in the isolation cabin. She suspects the director *wants* to make a scene about it.

"Come on," Lexie orders, as they clear their dirty dishes from the table. "Let's go finish our barge!"

Happy to get away from all of the attention, their group escapes to the craft hut in the woods. Ally glues the stick on that she found that morning, and they all add some final touches.

"All done, except for the candle and the holder for it," Lexie declares. "We won't get that until tomorrow, though."

"Can we go swimming now?" Becky asks, looking at everyone hopefully. "I want to show Sam and Ally what I learned."

They all quickly agree that it's a good idea, and spend the rest of their free time at the pool. With the sun shining down on all of the laughing, happy girls, Ally almost forgets that they have to leave.

Sam notices her best friend's mood change, and sits down beside her at the edge of the pool. Dangling their feet in the water, they sit silently for a minute.

"Do you think our parents will ever let us do anything together again?" Sam finally asks, looking sideways at Ally.

"They'll believe us," Ally says with confidence. "If we have to, we can get ahold of Sandy and have her dad talk to them. They know we would never do those things," she insists, kicking at the water.

Ally's anger is contagious, and Sam finally allows herself to experience the emotions she's been holding back.

"We might have one more chance to get some answers," Sam says. Looking around to see who's nearby, she lowers her voice. "Tonight. At the trailhead at midnight."

"You mean the meeting between Zorro and Ranger?" Ally questions, her eyes sparkling.

Sam is surprised to find Ally so willing, knowing she is normally the levelheaded and cautious one

"Yeah. If we can find out for sure what

they're up to, it might give us some proof. If we can find Cowboy in the morning before we leave and talk with him about everything, I bet he could help."

"Well...why not?" Ally shrugs. "What are they going to do if we get caught, send us home?" Laughing now, they hug each other just as the whistles blow, signaling the end of swim time.

***

Lexie was right. That night the bonfire is lit early so that the older campers can gather at dusk. Butterfingers announces that bedtime is extended to whenever the fire burns out. They start into several energetic campfire songs.

Breaking off later into smaller groups, they play various games before making s'mores and banana boats. Sam's never had the latter, which involves stuffing a banana with chocolate and marshmallows, wrapping it in tinfoil, and tossing it next to the fire to cook. Someone even produces cans of whipped cream to top them off.

By eleven thirty, a few girls have gone to

bed, but most are still scattered around the clearing. One counselor has a guitar and the crowd around her has been steadily growing.

When Lexie starts another ghost story, Sam sees their opportunity to leave. "I'm beat," she says casually, yawning as she stands. "I think I'm going to head out."

"Me too," Ally adds, standing with her.

Lexie only pauses in her storytelling and gives them a little nod. Breathing a sigh of relief when no one asks to join them, she and Ally link arms and quickly walk away.

They had discussed the plan with their friends earlier, and it was decided that it would best for the two of them to go alone. Sam was adamant that no one else take a chance of getting into trouble. The other girls agree to cover for them, if it's possible to do it without lying. Sam hopes to be back before they're missed, so it shouldn't be an issue.

As they reach the edge of the courtyard, the sound of a car door slamming makes them stop before they clear the trees. A loud engine roars to life and then Zorro's truck passes within ten feet of them and they can clearly see Ms.

Cooper in the passenger seat. As it disappears up the gravel road, Sam and Ally stare at each other.

"So she *is* part of whatever they're doing up there!" Sam acknowledges. "Come on! If we hurry, we can still be there close to midnight. The foot trail has to be a more direct route."

Grabbing Sam's arm, Ally stares hard at her friend. "Are you sure about this?" she demands. "This might be more serious than we realize. Maybe we should wait and just tell our parents in the morning." Now that Ally's sharp edge of anger from earlier has worn off, the reasonable side of her is winning over.

"Tell them what?" Sam counters. "We have a lot of suspicions and some weird things have happened to us, but we don't have any real explanations as to *why*. What if they think we're trying to make excuses?"

Ally considers this for a minute. She knows that Sam would never push her too hard to do something she didn't want to do. If she says she doesn't want to go, then Sam won't go either. *But* – "Okay," she finally decides. "But let's just see what it is they've got going on, and then come back. Right?"

"Right," Sam confirms, anxious to get going.

"Come on then," Ally urges. "We'd better hurry."

Stopping briefly at the cabin for their flashlights, they take off up the trail at a jog.

Over half an hour later, Sam is just beginning to wonder if they somehow got lost, when she finally recognizes a small meadow. The woods seem otherworldly in the bright moonlight. The sounds and smells are so different from during the day.

On the far side of the meadow, Sam signals for Ally to turn her flashlight off, and then they creep as quietly as they can around the next bend. The open space that houses the horses comes into view, and as they expected, Zorro's truck is already there. It's only a few minutes past midnight though, so they're hopeful that they made it in time.

"He's late," Ms. Cooper says loudly from the dark recesses of a nearby shed.

Ally slams into Sam's back when she freezes at the sound, and both of them nearly fall to the forest floor. Kneeling down, they hold onto each other and wait to see if they were heard, but the conversation continues uninterrupted.

"What's new?" Zorro answers. Pinecones crunch underfoot as he emerges from the shed and walks over to his truck, not even twenty feet away from where Sam and Ally are crouched behind a tree. "I don't even know why you bothered to come," he adds.

"I told you," Ms. Cooper answers, obviously irritated. "I need to speak with both of you *tonight*. Are you sure we can trust Ranger not to talk to anyone?" she asks, her tone changing to one of concern.

"He'll do what I tell him," Zorro says darkly. At the sound of distant hoof beats, he turns on the truck's headlights.

Ranger and the three horses left behind earlier soon come into view, each with metal barrels strapped to their backs.

"It's about time," Zorro barks, pushing away from the pickup. He starts yanking at the ropes and releasing the loads.

"I spent *hours* trying to find that stupid container," Ranger whines.

"You didn't find it?" Zorro yells. "How hard can it be?"

"They float when they're empty, man," Ranger complains. "We got to figure a new way to dump that stuff, 'cause this ain't working. And I think I need a mask or something, because it gave me a headache last time. I don't like breathing it, man…it *stinks*."

"None of that matters anymore," Ms. Cooper announces. Ranger becomes noticeably agitated when he sees her for the first time.

"What are you talking about?" Zorro asks, pausing in his task.

"I'm talking about the risk outweighing the benefit," the older woman scolds. "Now that I've got things set up with Mr. Hollingsworth, I can't take any unnecessary chances. After he hears about the incident with his daughter and her cabin mates, I expect to receive another phone call. When I put Hollingsworth in front of the board to rant, combined with enrollment for the last summer session being at a record low, my sisters will have no choice but to listen to me and your father, Zorro."

Sam and Ally look at each other, wide-eyed, their faces slightly illuminated by the moonlight filtering through the cedar boughs. *You were right!* Ally mouths silently, and Sam nods in understanding.

"Not having to pay to legally dump this stuff is saving us *thousands* of dollars a month!" Zorro counters, turning to face his aunt. "Besides, this is our property. It's nobody else's business what we do with it."

"You know, you're as smart as your father," Ms. Cooper says sarcastically. "The toxins you're dumping in the water are flowing *downstream* into a national forest! Mr. Hollingsworth is an intelligent businessman, and it wouldn't take much for him to put it together, and then the deal would be off. Besides, those two snoopy girls are onto us…I just know it. They served their purpose, and I'm getting rid of them, but we need to have *all* evidence of this gone before the morning, just in case their parents believe them. Got it? *All* of it!"

Ranger starts whining again, and Sam motions to Ally to back away. They've heard enough, and she's anxious to get back to camp before they're missed. As they slowly begin their retreat, a familiar voice calls out from behind them!

Spinning around in alarm, Sam is relieved to find that it's Butterfingers. "Thank goodness!" she cries, stumbling towards her. "We need to get back to camp and find Nurse Pine!" Sam figures that the other board member will be their most likely ally, since Cowboy hasn't returned from town yet.

"Now why would I want to do that?" Butterfingers asks coyly. "Zorro!" she calls out, smirking at the two astonished girls. "I've got a present for you."

19

THE TRUTH WON'T SET YOU FREE

"You two are either really brave, or just very stupid," Zorro states, shaking his head. With two flashlights aimed at them, Sam and Ally have no choice but to step forward, with Butterfingers herding them from behind.

"I think it's a combination of both," Ms. Cooper observes, hands on her hips. "You should have let this go," she cautions, her voice low and dangerous. "But you don't know when it's best to just mind your own business, do you? Well, you're about to learn a big lesson."

Not liking the sound of *that*, Sam latches

on to the hand that Ally has clamped over her arm. They crowd against each other as the space between them and the three adults narrows.

"Good job, Babe," Zorro says to Butterfingers.

Babe? Sam thinks, looking back and forth between the two. "Oh no," she moans under her breath. The two of them are obviously a couple. "So it was you all along?" she asks, turning to Butterfingers. "*You* were the one sabotaging us?"

"You guys think you're so smart," the counselor sneers. "It was too easy."

"But we thought you were our friend," Ally pleads. "How can you be a part of this?"

A brief look of regret tugs at the counselor's features, but she quickly pushes any feeling of remorse aside. "You have *no* idea what you've gotten into," she counters, looking at each of them.

"And they aren't going to," Ms. Cooper warns. "Ranger!" she shouts, bending to pick up the ropes that Zorro just untied from the barrels. "Put each of them on a horse and tie them to it. Make sure the ropes are nice and tight."

"Ah...." Ranger groans, clearly unhappy

with the plan. "I didn't sign on to be no kidnapper!"

"Don't be ridiculous!" Ms. Cooper says to the cowering man. "You're just going to take them out to the trail ride camp for the night. You'll bring them back here in the morning and let them go. I'll explain to their parents how they ran away because they were upset that they'd been expelled. By then, we'll have everything cleaned up and anything related to this, out of my office. It will be strictly their word against all of ours."

"You won't get away with this!" Sam shouts, sounding much more courageous than she feels. Looking around in desperation, she weighs the possibility of being able to outrun their captors.

Stepping in close, Ms. Cooper crouches down to eye-level with Sam. Her green eyes look black in the dark, and her white teeth flash as she grins broadly. "Of course we will! You're both known troublemakers, my dear, and everyone at camp will attest to the fact that you were upset today. No one would dare doubt us!"

Sam's stomach is hurting again. She has a

sinking feeling that Ms. Cooper could be right. Thinking about how the whole story would sound, they might end up in *more* trouble.

Sam is thankful when Cooper leans away from her, so she can start breathing again. But then the older woman turns and hands the rope out expectantly to Ranger. He hesitates, but eventually gives in and takes it. As he approaches them, Ally starts to cry.

"Please don't," she begs, as he starts pushing them towards the horses. "We won't tell anyone, I promise!"

"Turn off the waterworks," Zorro jeers cruelly. "It's too late for that now. No one cares."

Not seeing any other options, Sam watches silently as Ranger ties Ally's hands to the saddle horn. Ally is still weeping, but Sam's face has hardened. Having come to the conclusion that trying to outrun them all would be a stupid thing to do, there's still no way that she's letting them get away with this. Her odds will be much better once they're alone with Ranger.

Doing her best to look fearful rather than angry, Sam climbs up into the saddle and doesn't protest when he wraps the rope painfully around her wrists, placing a bandana under it to avoid leaving any marks. Zorro double-checks the bindings before giving his approval, but then adds one more rope, tying Sam's right foot to the stirrup.

"For good measure," he explains, winking at her.

Biting her tongue, Sam swallows down a smart remark and instead stares straight ahead. Laughing, Zorro goes back to where his aunt is standing, and starts loading the empty barrels into the back of his truck.

"Remember, Ranger," Ms. Cooper says, as he gets onto his own horse. "Have them back here and released just after sunrise. I'll be sending a search party out then, before their parents are due to arrive at 7:30. That way they'll be 'found' and back at camp right around the same time. Then I want you to go back and *get* that barrel! Understand? I don't want to see you again until you can tell me that it's hidden somewhere that no one will find it."

"What if someone sees me?" Ranger asks, understandably worried about his role in the scheme.

"I'm going to tell everyone that I'm sending you out to look tonight, as soon as the girls' disappearance is discovered. It would make the most sense, since you know the trails so well and already have some horses stored up here. Cowboy would be the only one to question it, or demand to go with you. However, he isn't here."

Smiling now, Ranger nods in agreement, finally seeming at ease with the situation. "Okay…yeah. I see how this could all work out. Just after sunrise. We'll see you later, then."

With that, he kicks his horse forward and Sam and Ally's mounts automatically follow. Once they're around the first bend, Ally does her best to twist in the saddle and look at Sam. "What are we going to *do*?" she gasps, the fear in her eyes visible, even in the dark.

"I have a plan," Sam whispers back. "But you aren't going to like it."

20

WHAT FRIENDS ARE FOR

Lexie knows something is up as soon as she sees Butterfingers and Ms. Cooper return to the bonfire together. Nudging first Sandy, and then Becky, she nods in their direction. It's nearly one in the morning, and they've been anxiously waiting for the time to pass, afraid someone would notice that Sam and Ally were gone.

As the two camp employees make their way around the dwindling fire, the three girls instinctively huddle a bit closer. Only a handful of campers are still there, the rest having returned to their cabins to sleep. Lexie looks around at who's left, hopeful that perhaps someone else is the director's target.

"Girls, please come with us," Ms. Cooper orders, slowing down just enough to make sure they all follow.

Groaning inwardly, Lexie scrambles to catch up, pulling Sandy and Becky along behind her. They look at each other fearfully, but know better than to say anything aloud.

Once they are gathered inside Cabin Navaho, Ms. Cooper tells them to take a seat and then eyes each of them sternly. "I have a very serious question for you," she begins, "and I expect an honest answer." When the girls indicate that they understand, she continues.

"It appears that Sam and Ally, being the rebellious children that they are, have decided to run away from Camp Whispering Pines." She's produced what's supposed to be a note left behind by them.

The shocked reaction from the three is genuine, so there's no chance of it being mistaken for anything else. "What I need to know from you," she continues, "is what they said before they left this evening. Did you *know* they planned to do this?"

"No!" Lexie is quick to answer. Trying to read the message, all she can see are Sam and Ally's names signed at the end. "Sam said they were tired and were coming back here. I figured that with everything that, umm....had happened, they didn't feel much like hanging out with us." Technically, it's not a lie since Sam really *did* tell them that.

"Well, I say good riddance!" Sandy announces, drawing surprised looks from everyone. "Seriously," she continues in response to their scrutiny. "They've been nothing but trouble. First, they almost got us attacked by raccoons, and then they plugged the toilets, forcing us to walk all the way to the bathroom at the pool. Sam couldn't even follow one simple rule. She could have gotten us *killed* on the horseback ride. Just wait 'till I tell my father about it!"

Lexie is almost buying the act, but then she sees the look of satisfaction on Ms. Cooper's face and realizes that Sandy is a whole lot smarter than she seems.

"Well, they might be pains, but I hope that

they're okay. Are you looking for them?" Lexie directs the question to Butterfingers, who's been very quiet.

Glancing first at the director, the counselor plops down on her bed, exhausted. "We've sent Ranger to go looking for them, but that's it until morning. It's too dangerous to do anything else in the dark."

"You're just going to leave them out there all night?" Becky asks in alarm, tears welling in her eyes. "What if they're hurt?"

"Stop being so dramatic!" Ms. Cooper shouts much louder than the situation calls for. "They are the ones who chose to put themselves in this position. I'm sure they're probably hiding somewhere, perfectly safe. I imagine we'll see them in the morning when they get hungry." Turning to go, she whispers something to Butterfingers and then slams the screen door behind her on her way out.

"Come on now, it's time for you to go to bed." The exhausted counselor doesn't even get up, and kicks her shoes off before lying down. "I promise that we'll look for them first thing if they aren't back by morning." Yawning, her eyes are already closed.

Looking at each other curiously, Lexie, Sandy, and Becky sit quietly for several long minutes, until the steady and rhythmic snoring proves that Butterfingers is asleep. Creeping carefully to the light switch, Lexie snaps it off and then crouches down in front of the two other girls.

"Something's gone horribly wrong," she whispers, eyes wide.

"We need to call for help," Becky suggests. "There has to be a phone here somewhere."

"There's one in Ms. Cooper's office," Lexie confirms. "But you have to have a code to dial out. It's an ancient system."

"What about 911?" Becky presses. "You don't need a code for that, do you?"

"I don't know," Lexie admits. "We could try, I guess. Wait!" she adds, remembering something. "There *is* a computer, and I know it has internet access, because I've seen it."

"I could email my dad," Sandy says with purpose. "He'd believe me."

When Lexie and Becky look at her skeptically, Sandy lets out a big sigh of frustration. "I didn't mean any of that stuff I said," she insists. "And I already suspected Butterfingers." When Sandy is met with questioning stares, she tries to explain. "Unlike you, I *knew* that I didn't put the food in Sam and Ally's bags. That only left one other person alone in the cabin that morning, after I left."

The three of them look accusingly at the sleeping form of the teen who was supposed to be their leader.

"She was in on it all along!" Becky declares, wishing they had caught on sooner.

"Let's go," Lexie urges, sneaking through the door, careful not to make the floorboards creak. When they are all on the front porch, they wait to hear the telltale snoring before heading for the woods.

"What do you think they did to them?" Becky breaks the silence, voicing everyone's fears. Stopping a safe distance off the trail, they gather together for support.

"I don't think Ms. Cooper is stupid enough to actually hurt them," Lexie reassures them. "That's why she's telling everyone they ran away. She must have caught them spying. I'll bet

Sam and Ally discovered something important, and Ms. Cooper is making them look bad so no one will believe them. But we can't take any chances. They're out there in the woods somewhere and we have to help!"

"I agree," Sandy nods. "Think about it. If they really *had* run away, don't you think they'd be calling the police and organizing a search party? No, they're covering something up."

As they try not to think about their friends alone out in the dark mountains, a slight breeze blows around them, stirring up dried pine needles. Tilting her head slightly, Lexie raises a hand and motions them all to listen. There! From high up in the pine trees, a sound similar to whispered voices drifts down and surrounds them, filling the night with ghostly conversation.

Turning her attention to the tree trunks near them, Lexie finds the plaque and points out that they're standing under Mr. Pine's tree. With a new sense of determination, they bravely find their way through the woods and to the back of the administration cabin.

"Here, take this file!" The familiar voice reaches them through an open window, and they automatically crouch down.

"What am *I* supposed to do with it?" Zorro asks his aunt. "I can't take it to the office. My dad would kill me if he found out what we've been doing." He doesn't sound very happy.

"Well then, throw it away!" Ms. Cooper answers. "This has all gotten out of hand. I won't risk it being found in our trash. I'd go throw it on the fire, but there are still several kids and counselors out there. I can't afford to do anything suspicious right now."

The conversation becomes muffled as the Ms. Cooper and Zorro move towards the front part of the office. The sound of a door opening and closing follows. After a couple of minutes, a truck starts up and pulls away.

The girls can barely make out the director as she walks towards her private cabin. Once she's out of sight, Sandy sneaks around to the door, but finds it locked. Their only other option is an open window. After some debate, Lexie climbs onto Becky's back and hauls herself through the opening. Sandy goes next with Lexie's help, and finally the two of them lift Becky in.

Going straight for the phone, Becky is crestfallen when there's no response to dialing 911, other than an odd beeping tone. "Looks like the computer is our only option," she confirms.

Sandy is already behind the desk, pushing at keys to wake up the sleeping monitor. "It's asking for a password!" she cries, unsure what to do.

"Try the guest log in," Becky suggests, coming around to stand next to Sandy. Clicking some keys to take them back to the main screen, their faces glow blue as the monitor casts light into the dark room.

"Got it!" Sandy shouts, quickly slapping a hand over her mouth. She lowers her voice and works feverishly, logging into her email account and typing out a desperate letter to her dad. Outlining everything that's happened, she explains that two of her friends are in grave danger and she needs his help. Begging him to come as soon as he gets the message, she closes by saying that it could all be because of him trying to buy the camp.

She asks Lexie and Becky to read the email before she sends it. "If my father feels that his actions might be responsible for someone else's trouble, he'll be sure to come," Sandy explains.

Lexie and Becky cross their fingers as Sandy hits the send button, hoping it will be enough.

21

UNEXPECTED RESCUE

Sam and Ally have been riding in heavy silence for thirty minutes, since Ranger yelled at them to stop talking. Sam is trying to ignore the sounds of the woods, which feed her wild imagination with terrible thoughts. She figures they have another half hour to go before they reach the edge of the ravine, where she can put her plan into motion. She'll need to figure out a way to tell Ally. Otherwise, it won't work.

To Sam's dismay, Ranger suddenly steers his horse away from the trail and into the trees, on a path that she can't even see. "Where are we going?" she asks, alarmed.

"We have to give you kids a full day of entertainment when we're on the trail ride, so we take the scenic route. *This* is a shortcut and will get us to the camp in less than half the time. Don't worry," he continues, misplacing her concern. "Your horses know where they're going. They'll follow me."

Her plot to escape now ruined by the change in direction, Sam looks around with growing fear, not knowing where they are.

"Why are you doing this?" Ally surprises Sam with her bold question. "You could go to jail for a long time!"

"I'm just doing what I'm told!" Ranger protests. "Zorro won't let nothing bad happen. This is all just a big mistake. You'll see. Now stop talking!"

Not wanting to push her luck, Ally wisely follows his order and they fall back into an awkward silence. But Sam can tell her friend's question rattled him and wonders if they can talk their way out of the predicament once they get to the camp.

For the next twenty minutes, they plod along at a brisk pace. Eventually, Ranger starts to pull ahead and Sam takes the opportunity to come up alongside Ally.

"So?" Ally asks hopefully. "Should we make a run for it, or something?"

"Nah," Sam whispers, shaking her head. "We wouldn't get far with our hands tied up. I've been pulling as hard as I can at these ropes and they won't budge. He'll catch right up to us. My idea was to-" Sam breaks off when she hears frantic neighing up ahead.

Straining to see in the murky darkness, she can just make out stirrups flashing in the moonlight as Ranger's horse begins to buck wildly. Confused, Sam looks over at Ally, who is starting to struggle with her own horse.

Suddenly another sound rises above the squeals of the mare, the same raspy breathing they'd heard the other day near the craft hut. But now, it's much louder and there is a new guttural roar mixed in that's making the hairs rise on the back of Sam's neck.

"What *is* that?" Ally shouts in terror, as her horse sidesteps and slams into Sam's leg, making her wince in pain.

"Get away!" Ranger yells, and then grunts

as he's thrown from his horse and hits the ground hard. The out-of-control horse stampedes back down the trail, its eyes rolling as it careens in between Sam and Ally.

The last thing Sam sees is a dark form stepping out from behind a tree close to Ranger. Then her own horse rears up and takes off in a panic. She holds on for dear life, but her horse swerves and kicks, trying to lighten its load. Her saddle slips to the side, but the rope tying her foot into the stirrup keeps her from being unseated.

The night becomes a blur as trees rush past, branches clawing at her body and face. Sam can hear Ally screaming from behind her as her own horse charges blindly. She finally risks turning to look back.

Sam watches in horror as Ally flails in desperation, her body completely out of the saddle, but arms still tethered to the saddle horn. "Stop!" she wails, her feet dragging on the ground. "Stop the horses, Sam!"

For several minutes, Sam fights to bring her mount under control. His neck is lathered in sweat, his side heaving, but eventually the horse slows. Using her knees, and pulling at his mane the best she can to steer him, she circles back to where Ally managed to stop and is now leaning against the saddle.

"Are you okay?" Sam demands.

"I don't know," Ally breathes, trying to hold back tears. "I think I sprained my wrist. I can't believe these stupid ropes are still tight!"

"Can you get back on the horse? We need to get out of here." Jumping at a branch cracking close by, Sam edges closer. "Now."

"Maybe." Ally places her foot in the stirrup and pulls herself up, wincing in pain. Settling into the saddle, she takes a deep breath and looks around nervously. "Which way do we go?"

Good question, Sam thinks, unsure of where they are. Her sense of direction is totally turned around, and there's no sign of any kind of trail. "I think the best thing is to let the horses lead us. They're more likely to find their way back than we are."

"You're probably right," Ally agrees. "Do you think whatever that was is still…following us?"

"I doubt it. The horses would still be freaking out."

Sam's horse takes the lead and the two friends keep up a nervous banter. They seem to wander endlessly in the mist-shrouded mountains.

"This might actually have been the best thing that could have happened," Sam observes, trying to keep the silence at bay. "It was better than my plan, anyway."

"Seriously?" Ally asks. She is slumped forward, leaning her chin on her fists, fighting exhaustion. "I can't imagine what you had in mind, then."

"It was risky," Sam admits. "I was going to try to charge my horse at Ranger as we were passing the spot where the deer trail goes down the ravine. I figure they've been using it to dump those barrels, so his horse would automatically go down if pushed in that direction. I thought it might be enough distraction for us to get away."

Staring at Sam for a full minute, Ally finally shakes her head in disbelief. "I hope that being caught in helpless situations doesn't become a habit, because we're not very good at getting out of them on our own."

Sam laughs in agreement, but her smile fades quickly as she looks around at the unfamiliar woods. They are far from being out of their predicament. She has *no* idea where they are, and the first faint rays of morning light are already beginning to appear.

22

REVELATIONS

"Sam! Ally! Can you hear me?" The voice is distant, but recognizable.

"Cowboy!" both Sam and Ally call out together. It's late morning, and they were beginning to lose hope of ever finding their way back.

"We're over here!" Sam adds, searching the trees for the older man. To her surprise, not only Cowboy comes into view, but also two other camp employees and a deputy sheriff!

Sam can't imagine how she and Ally must look: dirty, cold, tired, and covered with scratches and bruises. In addition, they're still tied to their horses. Earlier, Sam had succeeded in breaking off a small stick in her mouth, while passing under a low hanging branch. With it, she'd tried prodding at the fibers of the rope cutting into her wrists, attempting to loosen it. But her sideways fall in the saddle actually caused the knots to tighten. Her fingers are now numb. *Ranger might not be that smart, but he sure can make a good knot,* she thinks to herself in a daze, as their rescuers get closer.

"Are you *tied* to that saddle horn?" Cowboy asks in disbelief, racing forward. His expression of concern clouds with anger as he takes hold of the reins and pulls out a pocketknife to free her.

Once Sam and Ally explain the confrontation from the night before, the sheriff immediately radios dispatch and calls for backup. This is suddenly much more serious than some kids missing in the woods.

Cowboy describes the scene from earlier that morning. Sandy's dad arrived shortly after Sam and Ally's mothers. Ms. Cooper had just finished telling them that the girls had run away, when Mr. Hollingsworth read his disturbing email out loud.

A heated discussion followed as everyone weighed in with opinions. In the end, the authorities were called and a search party was organized. The sheriff's department determined that they couldn't take any other action until the girls were found and their side of the story heard. The police seemed inclined to believe Ms. Cooper at first, but that changed quickly when the officer saw the two supposed 'trouble makers' tied to their horses, exhausted.

Now that Sam has a chance to explain, she produces the label from her back pocket as evidence that Zorro's company is illegally dumping material. She describes the conversation the girls overheard.

The officer makes a second radio call, asking another officer to search the creek for the missing barrel. The authorities are not as quick to believe the Bigfoot encounter, but they add looking for Ranger to their list.

Over an hour later, the weary group finally arrives back at Camp Whispering Pines. They step into the courtyard just in time to see the police leading Ms. Cooper and Zorro towards the administration office. Both of them are handcuffed!

"That camp counselor broke down and confessed to everything when she heard you found them tied to the horses," one of the officers tells the sheriff. "It backs up those other girls' stories, so we've taken these two into custody for kidnapping."

"I have a feeling there are going to be several more charges added to that," the sheriff replies, looking accusingly at the conspirators.

"Kidnapping!" Sam turns to see Nurse Pine emerge from her first aid station, looking pale and frightened. "Katie," she moans, approaching Ms. Cooper. "What have you done?"

"Yes, please tell us. We'd *all* like to know what it is that you've done," a new voice demands.

Sam assumes correctly that this statement comes from Sandy's father, an imposing, middle-aged man who has just reached the bottom steps of the main lodge. Gathered behind him are the rest of the Cabin Navaho campers. Sam quickly spots two other familiar faces.

"Mom!" Ally shouts, running towards the group.

Sam doesn't know where Ally has found the strength to run. A brisk walk is all that Sam's able to muster. Her mom meets her halfway and gathers her up in a strong embrace.

"I'm sorry, Mom," she manages to get out, before being overcome with emotion.

"It's okay, Samantha," she sooths. "We know the truth."

"The truth?" Nurse Pine echoes. Continuing to block the way to the office, she confronts her sister. "Then what those kids said this morning was *true?*" She had been a part of the early meeting, and like the police, it had been much more...*pleasant* to believe her sister.

"Oh stop acting so shocked!" Ms. Cooper counters, somehow still managing to be intimidating, even though she's in cuffs.

"Of course, I know that you've wanted to sell the camp since Father passed away, but *this?*" Nurse Pine implores, spreading her hands wide. "How could you do it?"

"It's easy for you to stand there and judge me, but you're only here for a couple of weeks a year! I'm *trapped* here year-round, Anne. I have been for most of my life! This place is sucking our father's estate dry. But even when Mr. Hollingsworth offered us a way out, you wouldn't take it! So I had to find a way to change your mind, and maybe give Sandy's father some advantage to cutting a deal. You left me no choice!"

"It isn't your choice to make," Anne answers sadly. "This is what Dad wanted, Katie. *This* is his legacy. Those millions of dollars were earned by him. As his children, it's *our* legacy to carry out his final wishes."

"Well, *I* don't want it!" Katie bellows, finally starting to show some emotion. Sam finds it weird to know Ms. Cooper's first name. It somehow makes her seem more human.

"When Mom and Dad got this place, I was just thirteen years old." Katie explains. "I was forced to come here as a camper, then as a counselor and finally as an administrator. But I never asked for this! Didn't you ever wonder why I took Mother's maiden name after she died? Because I don't *want* to be a Pine.

"When Dad had his heart attack, I thought

I could finally move on with my life. But he made sure *that* could never happen, didn't he?" Ms. Cooper erupts into a weird, almost hysterical laugh, and staggers towards her sister. "All that money, but we aren't allowed to *touch* it!"

"Katie, I won't stand here and tolerate you talking poorly of Mr. Pine," Cowboy interrupts. "I pretty much helped raise you, so you had better listen up. You were given the same opportunities as your brother and sisters. You had an easy life. Mr. Pine tried to do right by you and pay for your education. But, unlike your siblings, you decided that college wasn't for you. You thought living off your parents until you got your inheritance was the easier road. Just because you didn't get your way, it's no excuse for all of this craziness."

"The irony is that her plan is likely going to succeed," Anne interjects. "There's no way the camp is going to survive this fiasco, and the fines that will be imposed by the state for the illegal dumping will likely tie the estate up in court for years."

"Oh, but you can't shut the camp down!" Sam cries, stepping away from her mom. "Mr.

Pine was right about this place. We need it," she continues, turning to face Cowboy and Mr. Hollingsworth. "Where else can girls like Lexie go, who just need a safe retreat for a while? Or kids like Becky, who would never suspect how brave and strong they really are without their friends to tell them? Or Sandy, where this camp is probably the only place that girls her age can see her for who she really is? Or someone like me," she pushes, looking now at Ms. Cooper. "Who came to realize over the past week just how much I have to learn about myself. That sometimes I can't do everything on my own."

Sam's friends gather around her as she speaks, confirming her statements and lending their support.

"Maybe there's another option," Sandy's dad replies, studying the group of girls. "I'm willing to let my previous offer stand," he announces, speaking now to Nurse Pine. "Only there would be a new clause written into it, one that would stipulate that the property remain a camp for girls, overseen by... err...Cowboy."

"Oh Daddy, really?" Sandy shouts, throwing her arms around her dad. "But what about your company retreat?"

"This is a huge piece of property," he says, holding her out at arm's length. "I have no doubt there's plenty of space for our own lodge on it. Except, it wouldn't be for my company…it'd be for our family. All this has made me realize the importance of the time we spend together, and we need more of it." Pulling her in close, Sandy hugs him back happily.

"Well, sir, I'd be honored," Cowboy replies. "Do you think the rest of the board would go for it?" he asks Nurse Pine.

"I don't think they're going to have any other option now," she answers. "And the offer is very generous of you, Mr. Hollingsworth. Thank you."

As the police begin to escort a very disgruntled Ms. Cooper and Zorro to the office again, Sam thinks of something and hurries to catch up to them. Ally scrambles after her, unsure of what her friend is up to.

"Zorro!" Sam calls, walking alongside him. Turning his head, he glares at her.

"What do you want?" he demands. "I don't feel much like talking."

"Your saddle bags," she says matter-of-factly.

"Huh?" he asks, confused. "What about them?"

"One of them has a hole in it. How'd you get it?" she digs.

Staring at her silently for a moment, he shrugs in bewilderment. "Okay...I'll play. I got it caught up on a barbed wire fence and tore it a few years ago. Why do you wanna know?"

"Because we thought we saw you in the woods by the craft hut a few days ago...making some odd sounds."

Throwing his head back, he laughs loudly. "Sweetheart, I might be a lot of things, but a Bigfoot impersonator isn't one of them."

Sam and Ally hang back as Zorro, Ms. Cooper and the officers climb the steps of the administration building and disappear inside. Zorro's laughter still echoes. Feeling numb, Sam turns slowly towards Ally and they look at each other in stunned silence.

23

BARGES

The rest of the afternoon goes by in a blur as the police conduct interviews with those involved. The investigation is kept isolated to the administration office. Since there isn't a present danger, the camp activities are allowed to continue.

Just before dinner, the officers assigned to searching the creek return with the missing barrel, as well as a very upset Ranger. He'd been found trying to carry the container out of the ravine. He'd tried running from them, but didn't make it far. His behavior, combined with the dying trees and fish, will be enough to launch a full investigation into the poisoning of the creek. When questioned about what happened in the woods, Ranger admitted there was something unusual, but refused to talk about it.

The mood at Cabin Navaho's table is a mix of relief and apprehension as the dinner dishes are cleared. When Sam found out what the rest of the girls had done to get help, she was speechless. Their friendship even stronger now, she knows they'll always remember this summer.

Sam, Ally, and Sandy are leaving that evening with their parents, so Lexie and Becky have been moved into another cabin for the last night. Sam hates to tell them goodbye, even though they've all promised to keep in touch.

"Girls." Looking up at the sheriff who's approached their table, Sam hopes he doesn't want them to tell their story again, or write anything down. "We've concluded everything that needs to be done this evening," he tells them. "You're all free to go. Thank you for being so helpful throughout all of this." Tipping his hat, he leaves them all staring uncertainly at each other.

"We should go collect your things," Sam's

mom suggests, "before it gets too late."

As they all head for the exit, Nurse Pine greets them on her way in. "Oh good, you're still here!" she exclaims, clapping her hands together. "I know this has already been an incredibly long day, but I was hoping you'd join us for the barge ceremony before you leave. It's a long-standing tradition here at Whispering Pines and I think you'd enjoy it."

Looking hopefully at their parents, Sam, Ally, and Sandy are all relieved when they quickly agree to it.

"Wait here!" Lexie calls to them as she and Becky run outside. They're soon back with a completed barge, the candleholder, and the slips of paper with their wishes.

"We finished it this morning, while we were waiting for you," Becky explains, her pride in the final product evident. The barge is impressive; everything fits perfectly on the huge piece of bark that Lexie salvaged.

Dusk is just starting to settle over the Cascade Mountains. The campers walk the trail to the lake, talking with excited anticipation of the ceremony to come. They're greeted by water smooth as glass, the rocks on the beach still warm from the late afternoon sun.

An owl calls out hauntingly from the opposite shore as they gather along the water's edge. One of the counselors gets into a kayak and paddles out, holding a long pool net, ready to scoop up the barges as they sink.

One girl from each cabin steps forward to place their barge on the lake. Cabin Navaho's campers unanimously chose Lexie to launch theirs. Standing in waist-deep water, her face glows as a lit candle is passed down from one camper to the next, representing the unity of the camp.

The barges slowly start to float away, and Nurse Pine leads them all in one final camp song about hopes, dreams, and lasting friendship. Linking arms, they form a chain that can't be broken.

Most of the boats sink almost immediately, the creators laughing good-naturedly when the lights are snuffed out. It becomes a game to see if one of them can swim to retrieve the wreckage before the counselor in the kayak can scoop it up.

As they begin the third round of the song,

only two barges remain, and then finally…Cabin Navaho claims victory when theirs is the lone flame flickering on the darkening waters.

Laughing and clapping, the five friends face each other, and Sam can't think of a better way to end this adventure. As frustrating and terrifying as it was, she wouldn't trade any of it for the amazing friends she made.

"This means that our wishes will come true!" Lexie says, smiling broadly.

"Mine already has!" Sandy answers, looking over at her dad. "It's funny, too, that I'll probably end up spending the time I wished for with my family right here!"

"Well, you all proved to me that I didn't *need* my wish answered," Becky admits. When they eye her questioningly, she shrugs. "I wished to be brave…but I found out that I already am, *and* I can swim!"

"You didn't need *us* to figure that out!" Ally assures her, putting an arm around her shoulders. "And you inspired my wish, Becky." When the smaller girl looks at Ally in surprise, she laughs lightly. "Sometimes, I judge people too quickly. I know I've probably missed out on some great friends because of it. You reminded me that I need to try harder, because you totally blew away my first impression."

"I'm not coming back to camp for the next session," Lexie says abruptly. "I mean...even if they get things worked out, I still won't go."

"Why not?" Sam asks. She knows how much the camp has come to mean to Lexie, and hopes that she'll be okay.

"My parents have been trying to get me to go on a camping trip with them," she answers softly. "Maybe it's time...to, you know, give them a chance. How about you, Sam?" she adds quickly, not wanting to give anyone an opportunity to make a big deal out of her revelation. "What did *you* wish for?"

Sam watches their barge as it continues to bob on the lake, the hypnotic chant of the camp song swelling around them. Turning back to Lexie, a huge grin spreads across her face and she reaches for Ally's hand.

"I wished for more mysteries, of course!"

THE END

I hope that you enjoyed, The Secret of Camp Whispering Pines. Please take a moment to leave a review at:
http://www.amazon.com/dp/B00SY3CPEY

Want to be notified when Tara releases a new novel? Sign up now for her newsletter! eepurl.com/bzdHA5

Be sure to look for Sam and Ally in other exciting adventures in The Samantha Wolf Mysteries!

ABOUT THE AUTHOR

Author Tara Ellis lives in a small town in beautiful Washington State, in the Pacific Northwest. She enjoys the quiet lifestyle with her two teenage kids, and several dogs. Tara was a firefighter/EMT, and worked in the medical field for many years. She now concentrates on family, photography, and writing middle grade and young adult novels.

Visit her author page on Amazon to find all of her books!

http://www.amazon.com/author/taraellis

Made in the USA
Coppell, TX
15 March 2020

16853719R00127